FINDING EVERLEIGH

A NOVEL

DONNA RODRIGUES

PRAISE FOR *FINDING EVERLEIGH*

"Donna Rodrigues links generations—and revelations—through the medium of a life-changing and life-affirming journey. Written for everyone who longs to wander to new beginnings, this traveler's tale investigates loss and discovery, the weight of the past and the possibilities of tomorrow, and the realities of uncertainty and new joy."

— D. J. Waldie, Author of *Holy Land: A Suburban Memoir*

"*Finding Everleigh* is the kind of book we can all relate to. Everleigh's quest to decide what she really wants, inspired by secrets from her past, sends her on a fun adventure through Europe, which is really an adventure of her soul. This armchair travel opportunity will inspire you to take your own journey both abroad and internally."

— Tyler R. Tichelaar, PhD and Award-Winning Author of *When Teddy Came to Town*

FINDING EVERLEIGH

A NOVEL

DONNA RODRIGUES

FINDING EVERLEIGH: A NOVEL

Aviva Publishing
Lake Placid, NY
518-523-1320
www.avivapubs.com

Every attempt has been made to source all quotes properly.

For additional copies or bulk purchases visit:
FindingEverleigh.com

Editor: Tyler Tichelaar, Superior Book Productions
Publishing Coach: Christine Gail
Cover Design: Michael Rodrigues
Interior Layout: fusioncw.com

Library of Congress Control Number: 2023900314
Hardcover ISBN: 978-1-63618-256-8
Paperback ISBN: 978-1-63618-257-5
E-book ISBN: 978-1-63618-258-2

10 9 8 7 6 5 4 3 2 1
First Edition, 2023

DEDICATION

To the world in which we walk through the doors of travel, both near and far.

ACKNOWLEDGMENTS

This book would not have been possible without the help and dedication of my husband, Michael Rodrigues. He supported me and kept me going as well as designed the book cover. I also need to acknowledge Mavis Lamb for helping me get my story from my journals; Tyler R. Tichelaar, PhD for his editing and encouraging words; Suzanne Brown for her keen eye during the final read; my sister J'Amy Gintz for her constant support; and my friends who always have encouraging words. And, of course my dad, Richard Elton, who is so proud of me for realizing my writing dream and making it come true. And, to Christine Gail of Unleash Your Rising for her coaching and support.

CHAPTER 1

Everleigh's phone rang just as she walked through her front door. This was not surprising since it had been ringing quite often lately. It was a damp day, as were most of the spring days in Seattle. The weather today perfectly matched her mood. Everleigh loved Seattle for its gloomy weather, rainy skies, and snowy peaks. It was home to her and had always been.

It had been like this for the past few weeks—the weather, her mood, and the phone calls. Her mother had lost her life after a fleeting battle with cancer just two weeks before, hence the sudden uptick in contacts and why Everleigh felt in no rush to be reachable. She walked into the kitchen to make herself a cup of Earl Grey tea, her favorite, and a time-tested comfort staple.

For a while, amid all the chaos that comes with a loved one dying (phone calls, sympathy cards, planning and hosting a memorial service), Everleigh became lost in the details, but now that the service was over, she was here, in the house, truly alone, for the first time since her mother had passed away. That phrase, "passed away," had always struck her as odd. When Everleigh was younger, she hadn't understood what it meant, and as she grew older, she felt people said it to soften death's harsh reality. So many ways existed to describe death without ever actually saying the exact words. *Language can be funny like that*, she thought.

As the mixed emotions and fatigue hit her all at once, Everleigh settled onto the couch with her tea, pulled a blanket over herself, and stared at nothing for a while.

The only sound she heard was the grandfather clock ticking. She sipped her tea and wondered what the next chapter of her life had in store for her since it was wide open.

Excitement was almost building in her. *Wide open...*another very interesting phrase....

When she woke, Everleigh had no idea what time it was, but the house was dark. She must have fallen asleep right where she had been sitting. She quickly remembered she needed to check her voice messages. She had been ignoring the phone for a few days while she finalized funeral plans. She had one last thing on her to-do list in that regard—to settle her mother's estate. Hoping one of the messages was from the lawyers who were handling it, she reached over and pressed play on the answering machine.

Something Everleigh had always loved was how her home seemed somewhat of a time capsule, originally belonging to her grandparents, then her mother, and now her. The grandfather clock, the carpeted stairs, and the rotary landline hanging on the kitchen wall all reminded her of the past. The rotary phone hadn't been used in years. A more modern, working phone was on the side table next to the couch, but Everleigh kept the old phone for sentimental reasons, just like she kept so many things in this house. She had grown up here, and maybe someday her children would too.

It was a lovely thought. Though Everleigh didn't know what she would do with the house yet—it was a lot of house for just one person—she felt lucky to have something so tangible since she was the only family the house had left.

Most of the messages were condolences, and she continued through them until she came to the one she had been waiting for—the message informing her she had a meeting with the family lawyers soon.

Satisfied, and still utterly exhausted, Everleigh pulled herself from the couch and headed upstairs for a real night's sleep. Tomorrow morning, she would begin to clean and organize things, starting with the attic and sorting through all the boxes and containers of the past. A past, it would turn out, that Everleigh barely knew.

The following morning, dust and dampness filled Everleigh's nose as she climbed the stairs to the attic. Even the staircase had a layer of dust from lack of use. *May as well dive right in*, she thought.

Everleigh moved the holiday decorations out of the way to get back to some of the older boxes and trunks. Some were marked clearly, and the contents in most of them would likely go straight to the donation pile; others were not marked at all. Everleigh suddenly stopped her sorting when she saw a vigorously taped-up box labeled: ***Susan Smith – Don't open unless you're me.*** Susan had been her grandmother.

The box had never been opened. With a tinge of excitement and curiosity, Everleigh grabbed the box and pulled at the tape; it easily gave way, being fragile after years of hot summers and cold winters.

Inside were bundles of letters, books, and photographs. Everleigh grabbed a book first, opening it to see not printed words, but handwritten journal pages.

The old, pen-scratched cursive writing was a bit hard to decipher, so Everleigh opted to look through the photographs first. Picking up the top envelope, she opened it and found some of the photographs were yellowed on the top, but surprisingly, many were in good shape. Lots of landscapes, buildings, bridges, shops…nothing looked familiar to Everleigh. Then she saw a young woman standing beside a bike in front of a café. It dawned on her that these were travel photos. Susan and

Everleigh looked much alike; they had the same deep hazel-brown eyes and soft brunette hair. They apparently even had the same affinity for cycling.

Everleigh continued through the pictures and flipped over a few to see that, sure enough, there were dates and locations jotted on the back.

How much time did Grandma spend in Europe? Maybe it was a honeymoon trip? She seems to be alone in most of these pictures…but someone took the photos. Not seeing anybody in the photos who resembled her grandfather made Everleigh even more curious. *She traveled abroad. Alone? Back then?*

At that moment, Everleigh came across a photograph with her grandmother and a handsome but older man. They were both laughing and looked incredibly happy. Flipping it over, she read, "John's Lane Church, Dublin, 1953," and at the bottom, "Anton at the chapel…details in the journal."

Oh, the journals, Everleigh remembered. Quickly, she began pulling the books out of the box. Opening them, she saw that each one had a date on the inside page: "*1953 – Ireland to Greece.*" She pulled them all out and did her best to arrange them in order. She checked the dates on the photos and found the corresponding journals. Everleigh flipped through the pages, scanning dates. Finally, she found the page she was looking for:

> Today was special! Anton has been so kind as to show me around some of the sights in Dublin. Can't believe I only met him two days ago, and we seem to be fast friends already. His fiancée is on her way to him, and they're to be married at this beautiful church within the next few weeks. Maybe I'll still be around or could return for the ceremony.

11

Still, it all makes me miss Roger more. I've re-read his last letter so many times. I do wonder when he'll be home. Enough of that. Tomorrow, I am traveling to Belfast!

That was just the beginning. From the volume of journals and the dates, Everleigh deduced her grandmother had traveled for a few months, and unless she found other details, she seemed to have traveled alone. *Amazing!* It was going to be interesting to read all about her grandmother's travels.

Just as Everleigh sat down and got comfortable, picking up another journal to peruse, the phone rang. She brushed herself off and headed downstairs to answer it, running into her room and grabbing the bedside phone after the fourth or fifth ring.

"Hello?"

"Hello. I'm looking for Everleigh, Everleigh Ford?"

"Yes, speaking."

"This is Stan Phelps from Wagner & Phelps Law Firm."

"Yes, hello! I've been meaning to return your call."

"Can you come in tomorrow?"

"Yes, I'll be there."

"Our office is in the Stanford Building on 5th. Do you know where that is?"

"Yes, I'll see you there."

"Great. We're in Suite 310. I look forward to meeting you tomorrow at 12:30."

"Suite 310, 12:30. Okay, I'll see you then."

Everleigh hung up, looking forward to having this meeting done. She would finally have all the information she needed to consider what to do with the house and settle the estate. Everleigh headed back upstairs to read more of the journals. Learning about her grandmother this way was so riveting; she felt as if she were traveling with her.

How bold, a woman in that time period, going off on her own like that!

Everleigh smiled to herself, thinking she and her grandmother must have been very similar. The same bold streak ran through them. *Must have skipped a generation.*

Her mother hadn't been adventurous or bold, and she had never really allowed Everleigh to be either, much to Everleigh's chagrin. Everleigh and her mother had disagreed on just about everything for all her life, and Everleigh had always thought there was no possible way they could be related because they were so different. Her mother had been cautious and quiet; everything about her life was routine, planned down to every detail, with no variation. Everleigh could not have been more different. She jumped at every new opportunity she was given. She loved nightlife, music, friends, food, and enjoying life. She thought life should be enjoyed, moment by moment. Not that she was irresponsible—far from it—but she certainly wasn't afraid. Afraid was the word she most often thought of when she thought of her mother. A timid, small existence cut way too short. Everleigh's worst fear was that she would go too, just like that, possibly having nothing to show for her life.

Everleigh and her mother had always gotten along, but they were never close. Everleigh had always felt a distance from her mother, not necessarily a coldness, but something was missing. Everleigh had started to recognize it when she was young, especially when she saw how other mothers and daughters behaved toward one another. For the longest time, she had thought her mother didn't like her or was disappointed in her, but she knew that wasn't the case; she and her mother had discussed their relationship several times, and she felt they had reached a neutral place a long time ago. But Everleigh had wanted more; she had known she could not break the wall down between them; it was where their relationship had been and it hadn't sat well with her, but there wasn't anything she could do about it now that her mom was gone.

Rummaging through these pieces of the past was like discovering a part of herself that was never allowed to be. It was incredibly exciting to find these items. Here was physical proof that she *did* come from this family.

Everleigh had never known her grandparents, or her father for that matter, so she knew very little about her family and where she came from or who she took after in the family. She sat back down on the floor, flipping here and there, reading in her grandmother's handwriting a list of countries:

Ireland, Scotland, Belgium, Germany, Poland, France, Italy, Spain, Greece.

Beside each country was a checkmark. Everleigh guessed that after each visit, a country was checked off the list. The last two countries, Spain and Greece, were unchecked.

She didn't finish this trip.

Everleigh would have to search through all the journals to know for certain, but that was what it looked like; her grandmother Susan had gone to each country except the last two on her list. Unexpectedly, Everleigh felt a sharp pang of hunger and realized she hadn't eaten anything since yesterday's service. She had been in the attic much longer than she had anticipated. Plenty of food was down in the kitchen from the countless care packages that had been sent to her home in lieu of flowers, plus yesterday's funeral service leftovers.

Everleigh headed downstairs to the kitchen to make herself something quick and easy. She felt called to get right back to what she was doing in the attic. It was the happiest and most excited she had been since the news of her mother's diagnosis and ultimate passing. She had been struggling to feel anything at all; mostly she just felt numb.

She had always been hopeful for a closer relationship with her mother, but now there would be no chance of that.

The finality of it all weighed on Everleigh more than anything else had. Everleigh had always wanted to be a better cook, even though her love of food was incredibly significant in her life. She tended to opt for easy fixes since they were less time-consuming, and she ate around her work schedule.

Maybe I'll take a cooking class and learn how to make elegant and luxurious meals. I suppose I should add it to the goal list.

The dream list.... That gave Everleigh the spark of an idea. She left her food, a vegetable stir fry, simmering in the kitchen and raced up the stairs, grabbing the entire box of journals, letters, and photos and bringing them back down into the living room with her so she could organize them by place and date.

Everleigh had figured she could experience her grandmother's trip in the same order she had, and a while later, with lifted spirits and comfort food in her stomach, Everleigh finished sorting the journals.

Luckily, her grandmother had been meticulous. In virtually no time at all, Everleigh had the journals and stacks of photos, spanning the entire trip from start to finish, laid out in front of her. She was surprised by the nervous flutter in her stomach as she poured over journal entry after journal entry:

> Today I start my trip to Europe. I'm thrilled to be taking this journey, and I've resigned myself to traveling alone. Mother's a bit bothered by the neighbors all fussing and gossiping about the scandal of me doing this. But I am surely not the only single gal who has ever traveled to Europe by herself. Just maybe the only one in our neighborhood!
>
> Who cares? If I stay here, I'll go stir-crazy with worry over Roger. The trip will keep me preoccupied until he gets home.

I can't believe he's already been gone three months. And, who knows if this chance will ever come again. Here I go, six months abroad, first stop Ireland! I feel so sophisticated!

She was sophisticated. You go, Grandma! Everleigh thought.

As Everleigh read these first few lines, she could feel the same sense of excitement her grandmother must have felt. How brave her grandmother must have been! Roger was her grandfather, that much Everleigh knew but little else.

According to the journals, Susan was waiting for Roger to get home.... *Home from where?* Looking through the box and dates, Everleigh gathered a few more clues. She found a letter from Roger to Susan dated January 1953, and a postmark from California.

Opening the letter felt a little bit like an invasion of privacy, but there was no stopping Everleigh now; she was too eager and curious to learn more. She was a curious person, and maybe, she realized now, she had always been curious because so many things had been kept from her—so many topics off limits between her and her mother—that only indulged Everleigh's sense of needing to know anything and everything about herself, about her friends, about life and about all the people around her.

As Everleigh read the letter and racked her brain for old history lessons from school, she began to understand more. Roger was in the army and was headed out to South Korea. The war was ramping up in late 1952, which would account for the fact that he had left three months prior.

Susie, I've put on a bit of weight, all muscle, of course, and being outside most of the day, I've developed a heck of a tan. I don't look like a 'fish belly white' guy from Seattle anymore. We ship out tomorrow, first to Okinawa and then on to South Korea. I wanted to get this letter off to you before we leave. I'll write as often as I can. I know this war isn't popular; likely, I'm not too popular right now either. I hope it's not the same with you. I believe I must do my part in this and hope you'll understand. I will serve my country, but then I'm coming home to serve you every day. I want to get married as soon as I'm home, whenever that is. I got one of the guys here to take the enclosed photo of me, so you can see how I look now!

Forever yours, Roger

She pulled the small black-and-white photo out of the envelope and saw a young man in army fatigues doing his best to look brave and strong. She noticed something familiar, looking closely at the crooked smile with a bit of a smirk. It was the same smile she saw in almost every picture of herself.

Going through these boxes was her only chance to get to know her grandparents. Everleigh relished the idea of learning more about where she came from and more about herself, really. She could dig, read, and learn as much as she wanted to know.

Her mother had always been somewhat closed off and Everleigh's grandparents had been gone for some time—her grandfather before she was born and her grandmother when she was just a baby. Everleigh laughed at being twenty-six and just now developing a special bond with them. As night fell, Everleigh reminded herself to get a good night's sleep and be well rested for her meeting with the lawyers tomorrow.

CHAPTER 2

The sharp buzzing of Everleigh's alarm clock stirred her out of her sound sleep. She knew she had gotten into a deep sleep because she'd had very pleasant dreams. Some dreams about her grandparents, Roger and Susan. Some about strolling down a stunning, nearly deserted beach at sunset. There was something so exciting about reading through the love letters of a man sent off to war to his bride to be, so romantic about a young woman in the '50s traveling abroad on her own, and something so personal about these two people being the very same people who were related to Everleigh. She felt herself fantasizing scenarios in her mind about them reuniting for the first time, the meals her grandmother ate all through Europe, what travel was like for her in the '50s, and how it would be different here in the '90s and how much of it would still be the same. Everleigh peered out her bedroom window to see that it was raining again. Not hard enough for a true Seattleite to use an umbrella, but enough that she settled on wearing her trench coat and riding her bike downtown to the attorney's office.

Everleigh loved these drizzly days (and there were many), though she was fantasizing about warm beaches and tropical settings due to last night's vivid dreams. Her mind began to wander, thinking about what life had in store for her, how things might change, and what she was going to do with the house. She knew the house was left to her; it was the only reason for the meeting this afternoon.

She'd never had to meet with an attorney before, but signing paperwork on her mother's will and testament was one of the final items on a to-do list Everleigh was all too happy to have over with. She spent her morning reading over her mother's will, organizing paperwork, and making herself look presentable. Over the past few weeks, Everleigh had not found her appearance to be much of a priority. She had always been attractive, but she was not the kind of woman to fuss much over her looks. She had medium-length, soft dark brown hair, hazel oval-shaped eyes, and a very warm smile that curved in the upper left corner into a little smirk. She stood at roughly five-foot-six, which she had always loved; she felt it was the perfect height. Not too tall, not too short. Her metabolism was still on her side at age twenty-six, and though a little curvy, she didn't worry too much about her weight, especially considering how she loved to eat.

Everleigh had always been a bit more of a tomboy than most, opting to cycle anywhere and everywhere, a ball cap on her head and tight-fitting jeans. She didn't enjoy that bell bottoms were coming back into style because she enjoyed staying in fashion only when it suited being able to hop on a bicycle to get around. These wide-legged bottoms that had been given new fashion life since first cropping up in the '70s were not cycle-friendly. She knew if she wore a pair, she would also have to bring spare rubber bands to put around her ankles to keep the jeans from grinding up the pedals and gears.

Today, Everleigh wanted to look like a pretty, young professional, so she opted for warm, business casual beneath the trench coat, her hair in a French twist, and a little makeup for good measure.

Feeling ready, Everleigh briskly cycled the several blocks to the Stanford Building. As she locked up her bike outside the high rise, she smiled to herself, thinking about just how many times her grandmother had been standing next to a bicycle in her travel photos.

Kindred spirits, Everleigh mused to herself. She found her thoughts continued to wander to Grandma Susan and Grandpa Roger. They were a great distraction from the anguish she had been attempting not to feel about her mother. She entered the lobby, and by reading the building's signage, she learned suite 310 would be to the left after the elevator ride.

The closer Everleigh made it to the front door of the office, the more nervous she felt.

Why?

Standing in front of the office door, Everleigh looked at a classy sign that read:

Wagner & Phelps, Attorneys at Law

She stared for a moment, took a deep breath, and walked inside.

It was a rather sparsely decorated office. A small waiting area with a single coat rack next to the door held a nice dark blue suit jacket. Everleigh hung her damp trench coat on one of its arms.

Her eyes wandered toward the middle of the office where there was an empty, but tidy desk and just beyond that another desk piled high with files. So many files that, at first, Everleigh almost didn't see the man sitting there with his head down, buried in his paperwork.

"Hello," she said, hoping to get his attention.

"Hi, there. You must be Everleigh. I'm Stan Phelps," the man said, looking up from the mountain of papers and quickly reaching out to shake Everleigh's hand.

Everleigh was taken aback at how young he looked, but she was also taken with his sparkling blue eyes and boyish face. Of all the things to be thinking about right now, she had not anticipated an attractive young man being one of them.

She could not remember the last time she'd had a crush on a man. She began racking her brain for memories of any time she had felt this instantly struck by someone. She'd had a high school sweetheart and a college boyfriend, but she was never boy-crazy by any means. She and her college boyfriend, Mark, had ended things four years prior when he moved to New York for grad school and Everleigh didn't want to go with him. At the time, she couldn't have imagined leaving Seattle. But things were different now; she wouldn't mind going on a trip to New York, or anywhere for that matter right about now.

"Pardon the mess," said Stan. "My partner's on vacation and my secretary is out sick this week so things are a little chaotic. But first, let me say I am so sorry about your mother." With his words, Everleigh snapped back to the present moment.

Right, my mom. The will. Think about that, not his eyes. Think about anything *but his eyes. Get it together, Everleigh!*

"Thank you. I appreciate that," she replied.

Everleigh never knew what to say when people offered her sympathy over her mother's death; any and every response seemed awkward and, in this situation, she did not want to give away her quick attraction to the man she had just met, so she stuck firmly to her polite thanks to move the conversation along.

Everleigh also never really knew how to speak about her mother's death. It had been such a sudden and unexpected event. She was realizing she was still in the denial or shock phase of it all; maybe that explained the numbness.

"Could you walk me through everything?" Everleigh asked. "I've read through the will, but I've never had to do something like this before."

"Yes, it's really just a few signatures here and there. You were next of kin; she left you the family house and a few other things. I'll explain everything as we go through it piecemeal."

After an hour and a half and a lot of signatures, to Everleigh's great relief they had finalized the last page of paperwork. Once they were finished, Everleigh began to shoulder her purse and stood up to leave, but Stan raised his hand gently to stop her. She felt hopeful it could turn personal, then subsequently felt foolish for that hope.

This is a business meeting; stay professional.

"Before you go, Everleigh, there's one additional detail we need to cover. We are almost done, I promise."

What else could there be? The remark piqued Everleigh's curiosity. "I thought we had covered everything?"

"Our firm has handled legal matters for your family in the past, including your grandmother. So, this is a separate matter, relating to her wishes."

"Oh? What were those?" Everleigh asked, very curious now.

"One of them was giving you this," Stan said, handing Everleigh a large manila envelope he retrieved from the top drawer of his desk.

"We were explicitly directed to give you this only in the event of your mother's passing."

"What is it?" Everleigh asked, eyeing the envelope in her hand as she took it from his.

"You can read it, or I can read it to you."

"I'll read it," Everleigh said in a rush, hoping not to sound as dumbfounded as she felt.

"My father started this firm; he's the one who worked with your grandparents. He said they were lovely people."

"I'm sure they were," she replied.

Everleigh sat back down, not knowing whether she should stay in the office or take the envelope to leave, though she didn't mind having a convenient excuse to sit with Stan a little longer. She also figured she didn't want a stranger reading this to her, even if that stranger was surprisingly adorable, so she slowly opened the large manila envelope to find a long letter and a few smaller envelopes inside.

"For Everleigh" was written on the outside of one of them. She immediately recognized her grandmother's handwriting since she had recently spent hours upon hours reading her travel journals. She pulled out a faded pink sheet of paper and began to read to herself:

Dear Everleigh,

If you're reading this, then both your mother and I are gone. I worry that you are alone right now, but I can't let that keep me from sharing what I feel I must. I'm extremely sick these days and worry I won't get to see you grow up; you're just a baby right now. I wonder if you'll even remember me. I wonder what your mother will tell you about me if anything. I expect your mother may not be as loving and tender with you as she should be, as she might have been. She's been cold, sad, and distant since she got pregnant. You see, she's been broken. I am not sure what you may or may not know at this point, so I will tell you everything here. When your mother was just a teenager, she was very sweet and naïve. It was 1970, and she went to her first high school dance, but it wasn't the dreamy evening she deserved. It was a nightmare. Your grandfather and I didn't think much of the young man escorting her. Unfortunately, we were right. Her date turned out to be horrible; he got so drunk he passed out, but not before he said some hurtful, rude things to your mother and embarrassed her in front of everyone there. It was so bad that Barbara wanted to leave right away. She didn't want to ruin her friends' evening, and knowing our feelings about her date, she didn't want to call us either.

So, she decided to walk home. It had always been safe for her before. Sweet Everleigh, I know no other way to say this…on the way home, your mother was attacked.

Everleigh couldn't seem to catch her breath. She seemed to already know where this was heading. Stan grabbed a tissue box and handed her one.

Lots of clients must cry in front of lawyers; he was a little too prepared for that, she thought.

"Do you know what this letter says?" Everleigh asked.

"I only know what I need to know, legally speaking. What's in the file and instructions, not every detail, but…"

"What?"

"My father told me a lot more; he was the one who helped your grandmother. I know it's all very personal, but would you like me to fill you in, or would you like to keep reading?"

Everleigh stared blankly at Stan. She felt waves of shock, anguish, guilt, fear, and sadness rush through her body and up into her eyes, where it leaked out in small, quiet tears.

"I think I'll save the reading for when I'm home," she stated.

"Your mother became pregnant as the result of a sexual assault. She didn't tell anyone until she couldn't hide it anymore. She was only a teenager when it happened and there was talk about adoption, but your grandparents convinced her not to go through with it and that they would be there to help."

"So, she kept me, but what does this mean for me? Why would my grandmother want me to know about any of this?" Everleigh heard her disembodied voice squeak out. She must be in shock, again. Her face felt numb and hot with embarrassment, anger, and confusion.

She had known about the young pregnancy, but not the circumstances of her conception. She didn't need this information since her mother had kept her anyway. This was not something she wanted or needed to know.

"She did keep you, yes..." Stan trailed off. "But...after the decision was already made to keep you, she found out there were two babies."

"Two...?"

"You had a twin."

"What? You said 'had.' Did they die in childbirth or something?"

"Have. I'm sorry; I misspoke..." Stan looked at Everleigh, expectantly. When she didn't speak, he continued. "Everleigh, you have a twin brother named Bradley. He's alive and lives here in Seattle. His name and contact information are in one of those envelopes. I believe all the information you need should be covered in that envelope."

Everleigh stared blankly down into the envelope.

"I know this is probably overwhelming," Stan said.

Overwhelming is a massive understatement, Everleigh thought. She could not think of what to do or say or how to behave at this moment. It was simply too much for her to take in. Everleigh sat for a while, and as she began to tear up again, she knew she had to exit Stan's office before she made a complete fool of herself. She was an easy crier and not someone who felt they had to hide their emotions, but she didn't like crying in front of others. Who does? Especially when you've just met the person, they are cute, and now this is the first impression they will have of you.

Everleigh gathered her purse, along with the envelope and copies of her mother's will, stammered as gracious a goodbye to Stan as she could muster, and rushed out the door, leaving her trench coat on the coat rack. She could come back for it later.

The last thing Everleigh wanted was to fumble around, trying to put her coat on. She felt Stan watch her frenzied escape from this bizarre situation.

Everleigh did all she could to keep from striking out into a run as she made her way out of the office, down the steps, and out onto the street, back to her bicycle. She didn't stop pedaling until she was blocks away, and she only stopped then because she was so out of breath she couldn't go on.

Blinking away her tears, Everleigh looked for a place she could sit down. Spotting a coffee shop across the street, she made her way to it. Once inside, she was grateful to see the place wasn't too crowded. She sunk into a booth in the corner against the wall as far away from others as she could be. Her heart was pounding hard and fast.

"What can I get for you?"

The server startled Everleigh with her sudden presence. Everleigh looked up to see a kind-looking older woman holding an order pad with the kind of patience that came from years of customer service. Her face had a few wrinkles, a friendly smile, and big blue eyes.

"What can I get you? You look like you could use something hot to drink."

"A cup of tea, Earl Grey, if you have it," said Everleigh. "That will be all for now."

"Coming right up."

As the server walked off, Everleigh finally took a breath.

She made an instinctual move to set her bag in the seat beside her. Only then did she realize she was still clutching the envelope, and it was a bit crushed from her tight grip. She slowly unclenched her hand and set the letter on the table, smoothing it out.

The thoughts just kept pounding in her head, one after another. They seemed so loud she wouldn't have been surprised if somebody else heard them.

"Here you go, sweetie," her server said, returning and placing a cup of tea in front of her.

"Thank you," Everleigh replied.

"If you want anything to eat, here's a menu. Our marionberry pie is amazing."

"Maybe later," said Everleigh as the server set the menu on the table.

"Just let me know," said the server as she walked away.

The warmth of the cup felt so good. Just holding a cup of hot tea had the ability to soothe Everleigh unlike anything else she could think of. Stirring in a bit of cream, she remembered the countless times she and her mother would sit by the fire and sip tea. They might watch an old movie, listen to the radio, or each be lost in a good book. Those sweet memories calmed her some more. Her mother had kept so much from her. Although, how would you go about telling your daughter she was a product of rape? That she was one of two babies? That she was the one you decided to keep?

So much of Everleigh's short life made more sense now, like why she could never get any information about her father out of her mother. All her mother would say was that he was out of her life before Everleigh was born and that was all there was to know about it. Everleigh had been so young that she had never really questioned that information until she was older.

There was a time when she had romanticized about who her father was, yet her mother's always hurried tone when telling Everleigh about him made her realize deep down that he was not somebody she would have liked to know. Everleigh had stayed up late some nights when she was a child, fantasizing about where her father was, what he was doing, and just exactly how he had gone missing. She liked to think he was like Amelia Earhart—hope always existing that he would be found, alive and well. Other stories included him being in the CIA and on a top-secret mission to help achieve world peace. Everleigh was a romantic in every sense of the word.

These late-night musings always brought her comfort and joy. She liked to picture walking down the street and passing her father on a chance encounter, one fateful day. They would know each other immediately, some keen internal father-daughter sixth sense. They would just *know*. Memories like these and more flew through her head as she tried to sort through it all.

Her mother's innate sadness began to make a lot more sense now as well. What a pain to live with something like that and never share it. What a deep sense of shame, which had never truly been her mother's to carry, but carry it she had, all those years. Everleigh understood so much more now—why her mother had always seemed so overprotective to the point of never allowing Everleigh to go too far on her own, and Everleigh had always been resentful of it. Her mother had always wanted her home, no matter how old she was.

Everleigh had always known she was loved, but her mother had kept her at an emotional distance, that was for sure, and there was never much explanation given to any rule; it was just the way it was, and to avoid her mother becoming even more distant, Everleigh had always reluctantly obliged. What was it her grandmother had said in the letter?

"I expect your mother may not be as loving and tender with you as she should be..."

Her server appeared at the tableside once again, this time with a piece of marionberry pie.

"On the house; you look like you could use a little sweetness!" said the server.

"Oh, that's so nice. Thank you so much," Everleigh stuttered as she fought back tears. She was surprised how this little kindness hit her so profoundly. It was a small gesture, but it was perfect and exactly what she needed.

Everleigh felt a mixture of bittersweet emotions, and she wished for nothing more, in this moment, than to be able to hug her mom again. She had so many more questions, and she knew the answers were in the rest of the letters, so she steeled herself to head home, open all of them, and read every word.

CHAPTER 3

Approximately an hour later, Everleigh unlocked her front door, stepped inside, made sure the door was locked behind her, and quickly went upstairs to change out of her wet clothes. After a long, warm shower and pulling on some cozy sweats and thick socks, she went down into the kitchen for some wine. She wrapped a blanket around her shoulders and made a fire in the fireplace. She wanted to be as physically comfortable as possible while reading something so emotionally uncomfortable as this letter, and she knew she would have to read it repeatedly.

Through intermittent sips of wine, Everleigh continued reading where she had left off.

Your grandfather and I didn't know about it for quite some time. Susan only told us about walking home because of her date passing out. She said her dress was dirty and torn because of tripping and falling along the road. I was sure she was keeping something from me, but I never imagined what it was. Eventually, she started to show.

When I pushed her for the truth, she broke down and told me everything. We had a good cry together; I can tell you. Your mother had been a virgin, and she was one of the rare girls in that day and age who wanted to save herself for marriage. After I explained everything to your grandfather, we all talked and decided to keep the baby. I won't tell you we didn't talk about adoption, but keeping you seemed right.

Then, at a sonogram appointment, we learned you had a sibling, a twin.

My initial instincts were to keep you both. Yet when your mother found out the twin was a boy, she was terrified. She was afraid the baby would look like her attacker, and more worried he might grow up to be the same kind of man he was.

She was terrified that she could not be a mother to him, so she refused to keep you both. She was so fragile that I realized it might truly break her. So, we arranged for the baby boy to be adopted. Your mother struggled with the rest of the pregnancy, and she wasn't sure she could even be a mother to you. After you were born, we found out she was suffering from postpartum depression—something they had only recently diagnosed and begun to talk about in those days. Luckily, she got treatment that helped, and she came to truly love you, but it was hard for her to be the kind of mother she wanted to be. The reason I asked for this to be shared with you only after your mother's death is twofold. First, I knew she had never planned to tell you, and I do not want to dishonor her decision as your mother. Secondly, your mother never knew I kept tabs on your brother. I made sure he was adopted into a good home and had a written agreement that after you were an adult, if you wanted to, you could reach out to meet him. He may know about you, but he has no contact information because I didn't want to risk him finding you before your mother passed. Besides seeing him at the hospital, I did get to see him one other time. It was after working out the details with his adoptive parents about the possibility of you two meeting.

They agreed based on the parameters I set. Before I left, I hugged him goodbye, and they took our picture. It was sent directly to the attorney's office—so it should have been given to you with this letter.

Please try to understand that everything we did, your mother, your grandfather, and I, was out of love. We weren't perfect and I know we made mistakes. Your grandfather and I with your mother, and your mother with you, but you will find in life that sometimes you do things solely for the love of others, even if they don't seem to make sense. I know I did that, more than once. Everleigh, I hope your life has turned out well. I hope you have big dreams and are chasing them. If you are not, please start today. Maybe meeting your brother will be the thing that puts everything in place for you. Only you can make that decision.

With all my love, Susan Smith Ford

Everleigh did exactly as she had anticipated and read through every page over and over. She had always done this when she was figuring something out, even if she already had the details in her mind; she felt if she read things over again, she would find pieces of information that had been missing the first time, pieces of a puzzle to put together, and in this instance, for things to make more sense than they did.

It was dizzying to have this knowledge inside her head now. What would she even do with it? *Did* her brother know about her, or had he been kept in the dark about things in the family like she had? What was he like? Did he have a family of his own?

Everleigh woke the next morning to her phone ringing. It was becoming a habit to fall asleep wherever she happened to be. She decided to let the phone ring to screen the call. Her policy was always: *If it's important, they will leave a message; if they don't, it wasn't that important.*

Everleigh enjoyed chatting with her friends on the telephone, though lately, she found herself wanting space, and she liked to be alone with her thoughts. The repetitive conversations she had been having recently were starting to wear on her. When the answering machine picked up, Stan's voice was on the other end. She felt silly about how she had left his office the day prior and hadn't been sure if she would speak to him again, or if she did, what she would say. Here was her chance.

"Hi, Ms. Ford. This is Stan Phelps. I wanted to call to check in and see how you were doing; I know that yesterday was a trying day…."

Stan had a nice voice; she hadn't noticed it before, but maybe she had been too busy looking at his eyes yesterday. His voice was sweet and gentle, yet still masculine and affirmative. It was very nice to listen to indeed. Everleigh picked up the phone before he could finish leaving his voicemail.

"Hi, Mr. Phelps. It's me. I was just screening my calls," she said more formally than she had intended.

"I wanted to touch base with you after our meeting," said Stan. "I know you are going through a lot."

"Thank you. It's very thoughtful of you to check in with me."

"Of course. Contrary to popular belief, lawyers do care about people, especially when they are clients."

Ah, so I'm just a client to him. This is a business call.

"If you need any help," he said, "after you decide what you would like to do with the house, let me know. I can help you with that paperwork, Ms. Ford."

"You can call me Everleigh," she replied, trying to sound a bit more casual but not *too* casual.

"Sure, Everleigh," he replied.

She liked the sound of her name coming out of his mouth. She was moved; even if he possibly didn't like her in that way, he seemed so genuine and kind that it warmed her heart regardless. She had not been so struck by a man for several years. Everleigh was the kind of person to fall in love with another's heart first and their looks later. This was the rare time when it might be both—not that she was in love, but it was an intense attraction, a crush, unlike anything she had previously felt.

Unsure of how to end the conversation, or continue it for that matter, Everleigh stayed awkwardly quiet. Maybe she could ask him out to coffee under the pretense of a business meeting and gauge things from there?

"Oh, Everleigh, there is one more thing…" Stan said, interrupting her thoughts.

"Sure, what's that?" *Maybe this is mutual,* she thought cheerfully.

"You left your coat in my office, and I was wondering if you'd like it back."

Everleigh's cheeks flushed bright red; the great thing about being on the telephone was Stan couldn't see it. This was so embarrassing. *He's a professional. He's just doing his job and covering bases. This is not a personal call,* she had to remind herself, but still, she felt a little hopeful that it created an opportunity for her to see him again where she could be charming and not a complete and total mess because she had just found out some horrific family news.

"I think I *would* like it back," she said as if it were nothing.

"How about we meet downtown, near my office sometime next week because I will be out of town for the next few days."

"That would be great," said Everleigh. "I'll buy you a cup of coffee in exchange for the safe return of my coat."

"That sounds great. We'll do that!"

Everleigh admired Stan for being so young yet having such a mature nature. She liked his professionalism even if she found herself wanting to break through it a little.

"I hope you don't mind. I tried it on, but a women's medium just doesn't fit."

Yes, a sense of humor!

"Well, you better not have stretched it out," she replied.

They set a date for Thursday afternoon next week for a short coffee break during his lunch hour. Everleigh hung up the phone feeling euphoric. This felt good even if it didn't turn into anything else. She knew she would like to be around him again.

Everleigh decided to transition to reading more letters from her grandfather, from his time in Korea. Most of the letters worked hard to be upbeat and positive. Everleigh could tell Roger was making light of things and didn't want Susan to worry. Back then, offering selected information was easier to do with less technology at your hands. Today, all the horrors of the Korean War were common knowledge, so Everleigh could only imagine what her grandfather was going through when he wrote those letters. Soon enough, she came to the last letter in the bundle:

> Dear Susan,
>
> I can't tell you how much I've been missing you. It's rough over here and I have to say I'm tired of sleeping outside. I don't care if I never see another tent when I get home, and that leads me to some wonderful news.
>
> I AM COMING HOME!

I know I've only been here seven months, but it feels like a lifetime. I am not sure exactly when I will head out, but it will be soon. Susan, you may have noticed the return address on this envelope—Okinawa. Please don't get too worried; I'm not hurt. At least nothing I won't heal from. I won't go into any details here, but it's enough that they say I can't go back out and fight, so they're not asking me to reenlist. My initial tour of duty is done, so they're sending me home. I've got some more healing to do before they can get rid of me, but I'll keep you posted. I hope that you'll be there when I get home. Seeing your face will be the best medicine.

Love, Roger

Everleigh had had no idea that her grandfather had been wounded in Korea. Of course, by now she understood just how little she knew about any of her family. As she held the letter in her hand, she reread the date on it and did some math. She then looked at the last entry in her grandmother's journals, which was after her grandfather had come home.

She looked back in the box for any other piece of information—another envelope of photos or something that might be the answer. She looked through the stacks of photos again and there it was, a small airmail envelope stuck to the back of an envelope of photographs. She opened the envelope and pulled out the letter:

Dear Susan,

Well, it took a couple of weeks, but I made it home. I was surprised to hear you're still in Europe. I know your initial plan was six months, and it's only been five, but I hoped you might change your plans knowing I was coming back. Susan, I know this trip has been life-changing for you. I imagine we've both changed a lot and will have to get to know each other all over again. I pray having a simple, quiet life will be enough for you, and that you'll want that life with me. I'm back, but I won't truly be home until I'm in your arms.

Your ever-loving, Roger

Tucked inside that envelope was a torn page from the journal. Everleigh noticed it had been torn in half. On the part she held in her hand, in her grandmother's now familiar scrawl, she saw just two sentences.

It's clear now…Roger must come first. I'm going home.

It seemed her grandmother had given up the rest of her trip, her dream, to come home to Roger. Now, the final two destinations left unchecked in Grandma Susan's travel list made a lot more sense.

Her grandparents had been married after they both came back to the United States in 1953. They had her mother not long after they were married—within the year, if Everleigh's math was correct—which meant her mother had only been sixteen at the time of her pregnancy. How horrible that must have been for everyone.

Everleigh continued to think about Stan Phelps' call since it was the only pleasant thing at present to think about. She was surprised by how flushed this man made her feel, and she was hoping the feeling would linger. Her desire to call him was partly because she had a crush on him, but she also felt the urge to talk to someone who knew all the things she hadn't known until the day before. How much had changed for Everleigh in an incredibly short time. *It only takes a matter of seconds for your entire life to change, doesn't it?*

The next order of business would be to track down her twin brother, Bradley.

There was quite a bit of evening left, and Everleigh still had a lot of organizing to do around the house.

She thought about her grandmother ending her trip early to come home and be with her grandfather. Thoughts drifted in and out of her mind; most of them involved the house, her brother, her grandparents, and her mother. She felt anger, hurt, and sadness for what happened to her mother, and somehow, a little hint of guilt mixed in too. She wished she had known before now so she could have had more years to process all this new, profound information. Maybe she could have even comforted her mother. Now, it was all just unknown, a completely new beginning for Everleigh, and she knew exactly what she was going to do with it.

The sun started to set, and a warm glow was coming through the aged windows; it was time to take a hot, long, and indulgent bath and turn in for the evening. Once in the bathroom, Everleigh let the water run in the tub until it was piping hot, set the plug, and let the water fill up to the edges of the bathtub. She lit a few candles and grabbed her favorite fluffy robe and a clean towel. Laying them beside the tub, she stripped down and stepped in. As the hot water rose around her, she could feel her muscles relax, and she did her best to sink into that feeling.

In the corner of the tub, she saw the small container that held sample sizes of bubble bath and bath oil. She chose the lavender scent and drizzled the oil into the water. The room took on its lovely scent.

"It's clear now...Roger must come first. I'm going home."

Everleigh's mind turned to those sentences again and again as she soaked and mused. She had made several huge, life-changing decisions in just as many days.

She'd read through those journals so many times, and she felt sorrow that her grandmother had never finished her grand adventure.

Everleigh knew she was going to follow in her grandmother's footsteps and take that trip to Europe.... *Thewholething is practically already planned out for me!* Not just any trip abroad, but her grandmother's trip, and what's more, she would finish it. It was the best idea Everleigh had had in a long time. It felt like destiny was calling her as she lay under the covers that night with a copy of the book her grandmother used to plan her trip to Europe.

Everleigh knew there would be updated copies available, but she would do her best to make use of the book in her hands. She could tell which pages were used the most because of pen markings and dog-eared corners, places circled, highlighted, and notes made.

The book would be Everleigh's main resource for planning her own adventure. She also had the journals spread out in chronological order next to her on the bedside table. If her grandmother could make this trip in the '50s amid all the whispers from neighbors, then Everleigh could do it now. With a glance at the list of countries and cities, Everleigh realized getting her passport would be next, meaning she would also have to find her birth certificate.

Finding it and, moreover, the idea of looking at it made her sad, her mind filling up with images of a brother she didn't know and a father who never really existed. Her thoughts turned to her mother's bedroom, which she hadn't been inside since her mother had died.

Everleigh hadn't wanted to go in the bedroom because she knew she would feel her mother's absence in every corner. It was a pretty, simple room with mauve wallpaper that had a pattern of little flowers. The bedspread complemented the wallpaper; it was cream with mauve-colored flowers, a bit of a ruffle, and, of course, matching pillows. Her mother had still been very young, but she had always had an elderly lady-like quality to her, which was evident in her personal tastes. Even most of her friends were older than her.

On the other side of the bed was a built-in bookshelf and a small chair with a floor lamp. Under an aged, single-hung window was the desk. That was where Everleigh's birth certificate would be. Years ago, a dressing table had been there, but her mother had thought a desk was more practical.

The desk wasn't fancy, but it was good quality. Everleigh had been told it was her grandfather's and used to be in the living room. It was the only piece of furniture that didn't match the cherry wood and mauve theme. She had never noticed how the sweet, feminine room was the room of a young girl, not an older woman. She never recalled any updates to the house beyond required repairs, so her mother's room must have always looked this way, even before Everleigh had been born, before this horrible thing had happened to her mother.

Her mother must have wanted to preserve that feeling of innocence in a bedroom that would not change, even though everything else in her life had. Everleigh knew she needed this hurtful piece of paper to take her trip. She started making her travel list. She had seen a sign about passport photos at the nearby drugstore, and it was as good a place as any to start. Just then the phone rang.

"Hello?"

"Everleigh? It's Sharon."

"Hi, Sharon." Sharon was her mother's best friend. "How are you doing?"

"I'm doing fine, thank you," Everleigh lied. "How are you?"

"I'm doing okay, considering. Wanted to check in on you and invite you over for dinner tomorrow."

"Sure, I'd love to come over for dinner; is there anything I can bring?" Everleigh wasn't really in the mood for company, but she knew she should go.

"Oh no, I'll take care of everything. You just bring yourself, okay?"

"I'll be there."

"Wonderful. See you tomorrow, Everleigh."

Everleigh hung up the phone while thinking about Sharon and her mother. They had lived around the corner from each other for what…twenty years? Truth be told, Sharon had probably been closer to her mother than Everleigh had been. They spent time together almost every day.

No wonder Sharon called; she's just lost her best friend.

Sharon and Barbara had spent most nights together, propping each other up, keeping each other going, sharing a few laughs, drinking coffee or wine, playing cards, shopping—all the things best friends do together. Everleigh loved Sharon's cooking almost more than her mom's, and she found herself looking forward to whatever dish she would be served tomorrow night.

Everleigh now made her way into her mother's bedroom, to the old desk, and began rummaging around until she found the files with "EVERLEIGH FORD" written on the outside. Here was a miniature history of Everleigh: report cards, childhood art that likely graced the kitchen refrigerator at one time, and medical records like immunization dates, plus a baby tooth in a small envelope with a note attached, "Everleigh's first tooth."

Everleigh had no idea her mother had kept anything like that; it seemed too sentimental for her, and Everleigh had never thought of her mother as the type to care about saccharine details or fond memories. Upon finding her Social Security card and her birth certificate, she gently pulled them out to take a closer look: "Everleigh Katherine Ford, Date of Birth: May 15th, 1971, Mother: Barbara Jane Ford, Father: Unknown."

That little piece of information stung more right now than it ever had   before: Unknown.

CHAPTER 4

"Bradley Langdon, Seattle."

Obviously, Langdon was his adopted name.... Everleigh wondered how her grandmother had managed to find him unless, of course, it had been an open adoption. She turned the page of her grandmother's letter over and saw an address that had been crossed out. Under that, in someone else's handwriting, was another address, along with his birthdate, the same as hers. She held her breath as she pulled out the white page listings and looked for a Bradley Langdon with the same address as on the paper. She was so excited to see he lived in the same city as she did. Everleigh got so lost in her search that she realized a few hours had passed and she needed to head out to get her passport photo taken.

As Everleigh drove, the sweet morning sun broke through the gray clouds. A few golden rays beamed through Everleigh's windshield. The warmth filled her heart and brought a smile to her face. The anxiousness she'd been feeling was making way for excitement. This would be the trip of a lifetime; though she was not certain how, she knew it would change her life forever.

Everleigh parked in the drugstore parking lot and walked in. As she made her way back to the photo corner, she wondered if anyone would be able to tell how excited she was. The more she thought about the pending trip, the more thrilled she became.

If this kept up, she'd be downright giddy by the time she booked her airline tickets. She walked up to a man wearing a generic blue polo and said, "Hi. I need to get a passport photo."

"Okay, it will be $12.99."

"Really? That's all?"

"Yep. The only place cheaper is probably Costco, but…"

"But what?"

"Well, then you would have to go to Costco."

They both chuckled, and Everleigh wondered if they had the same picture in their head—the massive parking lot with no parking, the clusters of people, the expansive warehouse, the hassle of it all.

"Follow me over here and let's get you taken care of."

Everleigh walked to a wall with a simple white backdrop. She followed the young man's instructions about how to stand and where to look.

"Now this isn't a fancy headshot," he said, "but it'll get you where you want to go."

"That's all I need."

"Where are you going, if you don't mind me asking?"

"Europe."

"Europe, wow! Okay, you're all done. I'll ring you up at the register."

The young man, whose nametag read "Josh," rang up the $12.99 fee, and Everleigh happily paid as he put her photos in a folder and then a small bag before he handed them to her.

"When you get back and have photographs you want printed, we can do that for you."

"I'll remember that, Josh. Thank you for saving me from Costco."

Before heading out, Everleigh picked up some toothpaste and shampoo. She wandered by the travel size section and looked at a few items. She'd always thought those little bottles and packages looked so cute, so she was looking forward to purchasing them.

Everleigh got back into her car and was about to start the engine when she stopped. She reached into her bag and pulled out the slip of paper with Bradley's address on it. She stared at it a few moments and then started the car. After backing out of the parking space, she drove out of the lot.

Almost turning right out of habit, Everleigh suddenly turned left. She had little trouble finding the small house tucked into the middle of the block. She pulled over in front of the neighboring house because parking right in front of her brother's home seemed a bit too much. The house was a small, one-story, white craftsman bungalow. It had black trim and looked like it had been a part of the neighborhood for years. She rolled down her window to get a better look at it.

The front porch was small but inviting. It seemed neat but plain, with just one chair on the porch and a few shrubs in the yard. Everleigh wondered if her brother was married or if he lived there alone.

"Excuse me, are you lost?" a young man asked as he pulled his car next to hers.

It was him. It was her brother, Bradley. This was not what she had been expecting at all! She could see her mother in his eyes and that same high hairline that mirrored hers. She had not thought beyond driving by to see where he lived.

"Yes, I do seem to be a bit lost," Everleigh lied. She was not prepared to meet him yet.

"What are you looking for? Can I help you?"

Everleigh noticed the paper with his address on it, sitting in plain sight on her dashboard; she grabbed it quickly and crammed it into her purse on the passenger seat, hoping he hadn't seen it. Her mind scrambled to know what to say:

"Yes, you can help me. I'm looking for my brother whom I've never met, who is you, by the way, and our mom just died; oh, and did you know we were conceived by rape?"

Turning away from her rapid thoughts, she managed to say:

44

"I'm looking for a place to grab some food. I'm tired and drove the wrong way."

"There's a great hole-in-the-wall pizza spot just two blocks away. I'm actually heading there now if you'd like to follow me."

Everleigh saw her chance and took it. "All right, sure. Pizza sounds great!"

After arranging details with her long-lost twin brother, Everleigh pulled into the parking lot of the pizza parlor and parked next to him.

She had known exactly which restaurant he was talking about, but she had to pretend she was hearing about it for the first time to keep up appearances. Everleigh could not wait until she could sit down with her brother and have a real conversation.

Just as Bradley was closing his car door, Everleigh bravely blurted out, "Need some lunch company?"

Surprised and delighted, Bradley graciously accepted her proposal.

Bradley took the seat across from her at the quaint, yet modest table adorned with a red-and-white checkered tablecloth.

Everleigh's mind was unquestionably abuzz; here she was sitting down with and about to have pizza with her brother.

Under any other circumstances, this would have been a surprisingly normal thing to do. As they sat quietly, she noticed their similarities; Bradley was well put-together, athletic, trim, and had brown hair—so many of Everleigh's same physical qualities. Maybe that was where the connection began and ended.

"My name's Bradley, by the way," he said. "It's nice to meet you."

"It's nice to meet you too; my name is Everleigh," she replied, relieved that the silence had ended.

"So, are you new to the area?" he asked.

"I've lived in Seattle my entire life," she said. "I just live in a different neighborhood, and I have a terrible sense of direction. I get lost easily."

"Me, too. I'm always amazed by people who can find their way around easily; maybe that's why I don't travel much."

Everleigh laughed a little.

"Did I say something funny?"

"No, it's just that I've never in my life been outside of King County, but I'm leaving for Europe for six months once I get my passport."

The pair, briefly interrupted by their server, ordered a large cheese pizza to share with iced tea to drink. To Everleigh's astonishment, it felt easy and familiar to interact with Bradley.

"That's quite a first trip," he said after she told him everywhere she was going. "I've always dreamed of going to Europe, Paris especially. What inspired you to want to go?"

Everleigh started to explain her trip in more detail. She thought it seemed like a good lead-in to tell him the truth about everything.

"My mother passed away a few weeks ago, and I've been cleaning out the house. I found these old travel journals in our attic that were my grandmother's from when she traveled to Europe alone, in the '50s. I want to recreate the trip since I never really knew her, and I wanted to feel more connected to my family."

"I can relate to those feelings; I went through something similar after both of my parents passed away. I felt adrift in the world."

"Adrift, that's the perfect word for it!"

Bradley sat a little straighter and looked directly at Everleigh as if he had something incredibly serious he wanted to say:

"This is going to sound strange, but do we know each other? I feel like we've met before."

"No, I'm certain we've never met, but it is very easy to talk to you."

"Maybe that's what it is," he replied. "Some people you are comfortable with right away. Anyway, tell me more about your trip!"

"Well, my grandmother never made it to her last two destinations; she came back home to marry my grandfather. Greece would have been her last stop. My hope is to go and see what she saw and more. To finish her trip."

"I've always wanted to go to Greece myself. There is something so appealing about it from the pictures I've seen."

"Me too. The water seems so bright and clear. I imagine sitting on a beach somewhere in Mykonos a few months from now, and that is spurring me on to be bold and adventurous."

More time passed as Everleigh and Bradley continued their easy conversation between sips of iced tea and large bites of warm, cheesy goodness.

"Do you mind if I ask how long it's been since your parents passed away?" Everleigh asked.

"A little over two years ago," Bradley replied. "They died within a month of each other. My dad first, and that was really hard on my mom; she just couldn't go on without him."

"That must have been so hard on you."

"It was, but they had a very strong and special connection, so I can't say that I was surprised."

"I wonder if it's harder for only children to lose their parents," Everleigh said. "You said you didn't have any other family. I don't, and I've been thinking about that a lot lately."

"I think it might be," Bradley replied. "I was adopted. I've always known I was adopted, but it was when I was a baby, so I never thought of my parents as anyone other than my mom and dad. Though, really, they could have been my grandparents because they were well into their fifties by the time they adopted me. They were great parents, but it meant not having them as long as I would have liked."

Adopted? You don't say.... Everleigh realized this would be a great time to gear the conversation where it needed to go. "Have you ever wondered about your biological family?"

"While my parents were alive, I didn't give it much thought," said Bradley. "I was well-loved and figured my biological parents did what was best for me."

"What about now that they're gone? I'm sorry; is this too personal to be talking about?"

"Yes and no," he replied. "When you and everybody else knows you were adopted, it comes with lots of questions. I'm used to them, and I don't mind."

Everleigh felt comforted by Bradley's openness and warmth.

"With both my folks gone," he said, "I do wonder about the remaining family I might have, if any."

"I can understand that." Here it was, Everleigh's golden opportunity....

Bradley gave her a small smile and then looked at his watch.

"I didn't realize how late it was! I'm sorry, but I have to get going."

"That's all right. Time flies, huh?" Everleigh said, trying not to sound discouraged. There was so much more to say, and so many things she needed to tell him, to ask him. She wanted very badly to explain exactly what was going on, and she knew every minute that she did not, the creepier their "chance encounter" would seem. Everleigh struggled to find the right words because all she really wanted to say was, *"No, don't go; we're the only family we have anymore. How do I know this? Well, you see, it all started with a dusty box in my attic and a manila envelope a really cute lawyer handed to me."*

"It sure does," Bradley replied. "I really enjoyed talking with you. I know you're leaving for Europe soon, but maybe we can have coffee tomorrow morning at Pike Place?"

"I would love that!"

He wrote his name and phone number on a napkin and handed it to her. She did the same. Then he insisted on paying. She waited by the register as he paid the bill. Then he turned to her and said, "We might not have family, but now we've got each other." He smirked and then he rushed out the door. She realized it was their grandfather's smirk that she had seen in photographs. It was her smirk too. Everleigh stood there, watching him walk away, dumbfounded, with the napkin he had given her still in her hand.

Well, that did not go as planned. She could tell him everything tomorrow morning.

The next day, Everleigh woke bright and early in nervous anticipation of delivering the news to Bradley. She biked to Pike Place, which, as usual since it opened in 1907, was just as busy as ever. Everleigh always loved walking through the market as the fishmongers demonstrated their crowd-pleasing antics, flinging the daily catch through the air to be caught and wrapped behind the counter. She locked her bicycle up and walked into the market. She didn't know where exactly she was to meet her brother since they hadn't agreed on a spot the previous day, and she wasn't even sure he was going to show.

"Hello?" she heard Bradley say from behind her.

Everleigh stood in silence, simultaneously relieved and disappointed, because his showing up meant he was open to getting to know her, but it also meant she would have to tell him the truth.

"Hello," she repeated stupidly as she turned around.

"Hello," he said again.

She was surprised he sounded so bright and genuinely happy to see her. She relaxed a bit. They bought coffee and meandered slowly through the market.

"So, remind me again what places are on your itinerary for your Europe adventure?"

"Ireland, Scotland, Germany, Poland, France, Italy, Spain, and finally, Greece."

"I'm really impressed by how adventurous you are; I'm not sure I could do it."

"I'm not sure I can, but this is one way to find out," she replied. Then, knowing she would have to tell him soon, she tried to start. "Bradley...."

"Everleigh," Bradley said, cutting her off, "I feel a connection with you; it's different from anything; I'm not sure what that is."

"Bradley," she said, relieved that he'd given her an opening. "See, there's a reason we're feeling connected to each other, and that reason might surprise you."

"Really?"

"You were adopted, right?" she said almost flippantly.

"Yes...?" Bradley responded.

"Do you know anything about your biological family? Your biological mom?"

"No, not much. A few details. I heard she was young."

"She was. She was a teenager, just sixteen."

"How do you know that?" Bradley asked, starting to sound defensive.

"I know that because...." Everleigh paused.

"Everleigh?" Bradley chided. "It sounds like you have something you may want to tell me."

It's now or never, she thought.

"I know that because she was my mom too. We are twins."

Bradley let out a small chortle. "What?" He sounded somewhere between amused and pissed off.

"We are biological twins. Our mom was sixteen when she got pregnant with us. Bradley, I'm your sister."

"Look, if this is a joke, I'm not laughing."

Everleigh felt very dismayed by that comment; even if they didn't really know each other, what kind of person did he think she was to tell him as a joke that he was her long-lost twin sibling.

"Bradley, it isn't a joke. I'm serious; I just found out myself after my mom, *our* mom, passed away."

Everleigh could see Bradley was feeling a little overwhelmed by the sudden information she had given him. There was stunning silence on both ends as they let the information wash over them. Everleigh felt scared that Bradley would just leave her—he was the only family she had left—but she felt some relief in knowing he now knew this secret. *It's done now; he knows,* she thought, but she also wondered how this information had made him feel. When she had first learned about it, she had run out of the attorney's office in a state of shock and confusion, not knowing where to go, what to do, or how to feel. She had never experienced emotions that hit her like a brick right in the pit of her stomach like that, even when she heard the news of her mother's untimely passing.

"I'm sorry, Bradley; maybe it was insensitive to tell you like this. I...I wanted to say something when we were at the pizzeria, but I had just found out myself, and I didn't know how to go about it, and you had to leave so quickly; then you mentioned getting coffee today.... I'm sorry; I should have had the courage to tell you then."

"No, it's okay. I don't think either of us knows the right thing here, but…I'm glad you told me now."

"I'm sorry about the way both of us found out," said Everleigh. "I got a letter at my attorney's office; I really wanted to meet you and see if you would have any interest in getting to know me as well, and I'm sorry for dropping this bomb on you right before I'm leaving to trek through Europe for half a year!"

Okay, well, it's done and over with now. He knows. This wasn't exactly the game plan, but he knows now.

As they sat there in stunned silence and drank their coffee, Everleigh knew someone had to break the ice. Everleigh took Bradley's hand and told him how she was so glad this meeting had come about and how she was looking forward to getting to know him more. He squeezed her hand and assured her they would be in touch and get to know one another better. With a sigh of relief, they hugged each other and promised to see each other before Everleigh left for Europe.

CHAPTER 5

Everleigh had to hurry to get ready to head to Sharon's house for dinner. She had been so preoccupied with everything else that she had nearly forgotten about it. Luckily, Sharon lived just around the corner, so Everleigh could walk there in a few minutes. She put on her good walking boots, which would keep her feet warm and dry if it started to rain again. It was too late to go to the store to buy wine or flowers to bring with her, which would have been a nice gesture for her mother's best friend. But she wanted to do something for her. Suddenly, an idea came to mind.

Everleigh walked into the kitchen and found her mother's favorite teacup and saucer. It had been washed since the last time her mother had sipped a cup of English Breakfast, her favorite tea. Everleigh hadn't been able to put it away yet, so there it sat on the counter. It was a much better gift than flowers. It would be a way for Sharon to have a part of her mother with her always. The slight knots in Everleigh's stomach from her earlier encounter with Bradley faded away as soon as she walked into Sharon's loving hug.

"Oh, Everleigh! I'm so delighted to see you; come on inside and let's sit by the fire."

The fire was roaring, and Everleigh caught a giggle in her throat as she took off her coat and laid it on the sofa. Sharon walked into her kitchen to get the wine, and Everleigh smiled as she took off the scarf wrapped around her neck and sat down.

She was glad she had stifled her giggle, or she would have had to explain what amused her as she walked inside the house. She had always teased her mother that Sharon kept her house so warm it was like a sauna.

"It's 'old lady hot' in there,"Everleigh used to joke. She wasn't sure if Sharon knew the inside story, though, and she didn't want to hurt her feelings.

"It's a nice Pinot Gris that will go well with the chicken," Sharon said as she came back into the room holding two large glasses of white wine, one of which Everleigh gratefully accepted.

"I've never been very good at pairing wine with food," Everleigh said, taking a sip.

"I just know the three basics," Sharon replied, "red with beef, white with chicken and fish, and always ask someone to recommend a bottle. That way you can blame it on them if it doesn't taste good."

"Good logic."

"Speaking of food and wine, I made one of your favorites, chicken Marsala."

"Really? That was so thoughtful. I can't wait."

"I figured it would do us both some good to have some comfort food."

Everleigh reached for the little brown bag she had carried with her. "I brought you a little something," she said, handing the gift to Sharon and watching as she gingerly opened the bag and peeked inside. She made a slight gasp and carefully pulled out the cup and saucer.

"Barbara's teacup."

"It seemed right for you to have it."

"It's perfect. Thank you so much."

Everleigh could tell Sharon was deeply touched to receive something so personal from her mother's life.

"I still have a difficult time realizing she's really gone," said Sharon.

"I know. I wake up in the morning expecting to hear her making coffee."

"It must be so hard to be in that house alone."

"Sometimes..." said Everleigh.

"I do know you and your mother had a complicated relationship," Sharon replied.

Everleigh looked at Sharon, unsure how to reply.

"It's like that with mothers and daughters, sometimes," Sharon said. "Barbara was a bit distant with her own mother."

"She was?"

"Don't get me wrong; she loved your grandmother very much, but I think Barbara kept most folks at arm's length. You remind me of her."

"My mother?"

"No, your grandmother, Susan. She was a wise woman and gave a lot of great advice."

"How am I like her?"

"Well, you look a lot like her; your eyes remind me of her. Some of your mannerisms, your voice, and you both loved Earl Grey tea more than any other. Strong-willed, bold, ready to take on the world."

There was a moment of quiet as they both sipped their wine and stared into the fire. Everleigh took comfort in being like her Grandma Susan. She wondered if Sharon knew how she had come to be born. Did her mother ever share that dark secret with her best friend?

"You're lost in some deep thoughts over there."

"Oh, nothing really; just thinking about Mom."

"Come to the kitchen with me and let's get some more wine."

Everleigh eagerly followed Sharon into her bright kitchen full of wonderful smells. She could almost taste the chicken Marsala and the herbs. Sharon had everything ready to go. She dropped the angel hair pasta into the pot of boiling water; then she grabbed the bottle of wine and filled both of their glasses.

"I've never been much of a wine drinker, but lately, it's been comforting. Someone gave me a nice bottle of red at the memorial service. Since then, I've had a few glasses every night."

"I've been having a few more cocktails myself. It takes the edge off the pain, doesn't it?"

"It does."

Soon, their food was ready. Sharon filled two plates with pasta, chicken Marsala, and garlic-roasted Brussels sprouts. They carried their plates and wine to her cozy kitchen table. Between bites, they talked about how good the meal was, about trying to cook for one, and about some of Sharon's favorite cooking shows on the Food Network.

Everleigh nearly inhaled her food, as she did every time Sharon made her a meal; it was great to be cooked for. She finished her dinner in an almost embarrassing amount of time.

"I've got dessert too. It's incredibly decadent," Sharon told her. "My own version of Death by Chocolate. It's not as many layers, but it's a homemade brownie, two kinds of sauce, whip cream—the works."

"I definitely can't say no to that."

"You can't! I'll start some coffee. I just love coffee with desserts. So, are you still off work?"

"I am for now. Sharon, there is something I need to tell you. I am going to be leaving for Europe soon, and I will be gone for six months. My grandmother went to Europe before she was married, and there were several places she was not able to go to because my grandfather came back from the war early and she had to come home. I am going to trace some of her steps and finish that trip for her. I am waiting for my passport now, and then I will be leaving. I am quitting my job and I will be meeting with my manager on Monday to resign."

Sharon was stunned and had a lot of questions. Everleigh knew it was a lot to explain in one evening, but she started to tell Sharon

56

everything, beginning with her meeting with Stan, and then the letter, finding Bradley, and making the decision to go to Europe. She didn't want to leave anything out. Sharon was a bit surprised to learn about Bradley, but Barbara had always been somewhat private despite all the years they'd been friends. Sharon really appreciated what Everleigh told her and her honesty, but she was so worried about Everleigh and what would happen over the next six months. She also knew Everleigh was strong and she couldn't help but be excited for Everleigh discovering her family and wanting to finish her grandmother's trip. Sharon would keep in touch with Everleigh no matter what because she felt like Everleigh was the best connection to her best friend Barbara. Eventually, Sharon and Everleigh settled back in the living room by the fire to drink their coffee and eat dessert. It was decadent and Everleigh thoroughly enjoyed the indulgence. The pair spent the rest of the night chatting away, talking about the European adventures coming up for Everleigh, sharing memories of Barbara, having a few laughs, and shedding a few tears.

As the evening wound down, Everleigh felt her eyelids getting heavy from all the food and wine. It was time to call it a night, although she had enjoyed it much more than she was expecting to. It was a great comfort.

"Sharon, thank you so much for having me; this meant so much to me."

"It meant just as much, if not more to me. We'll do this again soon after you return from Europe, and then you can tell me all about your adventures. But it looks like you're about to fall asleep right now."

"You fed me too well; I'll have to head out before I do!"

Upon saying goodnight, Everleigh gave Sharon a tight hug. Then she waved goodbye as she headed out the door and down the sidewalk. The temperature had dropped a bit, so she picked up her pace to get home a little faster. She really had accomplished a lot in very little time, meeting with the lawyers, finding a long-lost twin brother, saying goodbye to an old friend, getting her paperwork and passport ready. She knew she really wanted to take this trip because of the lightning speed with which she had accomplished all these tasks this week. Monday she would quit her job, and then there would be just one thing left to do before she headed off on the biggest adventure of her life, and that was to meet up with Stan to get her trench coat back, though really, she just wanted to see if something special was there before she left. She still could not believe she was leaving for Europe in only a few short weeks!

CHAPTER 6

Everleigh was nervously and excitedly anticipating her coffee "date" with Stan Phelps.

She was thinking of his blue eyes, his gentle voice, and his kind heart. *Wow, I really have a thing for this guy*, she thought. *He's just a man. Don't get ahead of yourself; you don't even know him. Act cool; be casual.*

She would be leaving for Europe soon, so this would be her last chance to see him for six months. If nothing else, she could at least gauge the situation. In their brief encounter and telephone conversations, Everleigh had felt a bit of a mutual vibe between them. However, she brushed it off as wishful thinking. She was not in the right place in her life to worry about this at all; she had a lot to do and a lot she felt was much more important than a romantic entanglement.

Hello? Seeing the world, tracking down your twin brother, telling him he's your twin brother, figuring out what to do with the property you just inherited, returning your friends' calls, quitting your job.

Everleigh arrived at the coffee shop after Stan. He had already ordered and was sitting down with a newspaper, a cappuccino, and her trench coat, in a dry cleaner's bag no less, draped on the chair next to him. When he saw her, he waved her over. She found it endearing that he was roughly the same age she was, but he seemed to have the chivalry found in older, refined men. Seriously, what twenty-something reads a newspaper or has somebody else's coat dry-cleaned? Where did this man come from? Did they make more like him?

Everleigh walked over to Stan and sat down. "I thought I was buying your coffee today."

"I'll let you grab the second round; how does that sound?"

"Perfect."

She nodded over at the server to come over to them and they ordered two more cappuccinos. To Everleigh's great relief, it was much more relaxed to speak to Stan here than in his office.

"You really didn't have to dry-clean the coat; it's too much."

"It really was no trouble at all. I was happy to do it, and I was happy to meet you here. I know what a difficult time this is for you, and if I can do some small things to make it easier, then why not?"

"You are very kind, and it is appreciated very much. So, tell me, is this your regular coffee shop?"

"It is. Since it's near the office, I'm a regular. I hate to say it, but I think I've become addicted to coffee."

"We certainly are in the perfect city for that."

"We sure are."

"I don't know what I'm going to do with the house yet," Everleigh said, suddenly feeling pressured to turn the conversation back to legal matters for some unknown reason.

"Ms. Ford...Everleigh, this is just coffee. We don't have to discuss that until you're ready to decide. I'm off the clock right now. This is purely a social call. I wanted to see you again."

Yes! He does like me.

Everleigh's stomach was flipping, but she reminded herself to be smooth. "I wanted to see you again too...."

"I'm afraid I have a confession, Everleigh."

"Oh?"

"I was actually somewhat pleased when I noticed you had left your coat behind. It gave me a reason to see you again."

"I see."

"Would you like to go out with me sometime?"

There it is! Everleigh was happy not to be crazy or picturing all the goodness of this crush inside her own mind.

"Stan, I would *love* to go out with you, but—"

"You're seeing somebody?"

"No."

"Sorry; that was presumptuous of me. You don't date lawyers?"

"Would you let me talk?" Everleigh smiled.

He laughed. Their eyes met. They had a mutual connection.

"No, it's none of that," Everleigh replied. "I'm leaving soon to go to Europe for six months. Otherwise, I would love to go out with you. I would say let's get together when I get back, but I don't know where either one of us will be in half a year. It just seems unfair to ask you to wait until I get back or rush into something days before I leave."

At this, Stan sat back and looked at Everleigh. "Europe for six months, huh?"

Everleigh nodded. She liked that there was a playful side to him too, not all business.

"Well, you have my number?" he said.

"Of course, I do."

"They have phones in Europe."

Everleigh liked how confident he seemed and that it didn't make him insecure in the least that she would be an ocean away for several months by herself. Plus, if she wanted to, she could just phone him. It was rare for her to meet a man secure enough to handle the type of independent woman she was. It was as if she had met her match. There was much to be excited about, nervous about too, but excited, nonetheless. One more night and she would be off to her first destination in Europe: Ireland.

Life was still seeming surreal to Everleigh, quitting her job, her mother's passing, her brother, Stan, Europe—but all of it was *very* real.

The day came and she was at the airport, Everleigh was carrying all of Grandma Susan's journals and some of her photos in her carry-on bag, wanting to travel as lightly as possible with only one suitcase and a backpack in addition to her carry-on. Her things were heavier than she had hoped, but she felt she needed all of it with her to recreate her grandmother's journey. She was quite proud of herself for finding her gate with only one wrong turn. The greatest advantage of being in the airport was that everything was clearly labeled everywhere with bright green or red signs, so all Everleigh had to do was be very observant and follow the directions.

The atmosphere in SeaTac was vibrating with energy. People were all around Everleigh, and every one of them had something to do, somewhere to be.

She looked around until she saw the sign she was looking for; it was the most beautiful sign she'd ever seen. The day had finally arrived, and Everleigh could hardly believe it was real.

She had spent so much time the past few weeks planning, deciding, designing her itinerary, packing and repacking, and making lists. She felt now she could focus on doing exactly what she had intended from the start: to absorb, enjoy, meet, eat, and simply be. To truly live in the moment, something she had never quite gotten the hang of at home. She checked her suitcase and proceeded to make her way through long line after long line.

Luckily, Everleigh had arrived at the airport in plenty of time to get lost more than a few times but not miss her flight. She bought a few snacks and a bottle of water at the nearby news shop; the prices were ridiculous. *Exorbitant,* she thought.

Good thing she had put away enough in savings for her travel budget for unexpected expenses. Although she already exceeded her daily budget today, this was probably the best Everleigh had ever done financially in her life.

She had worked the same administrative job straight out of college and never left it. Everleigh loved the people she worked with, but not necessarily the job. She never took sick time or vacation days so her job paid her out for them when she gave notice and quit. Everything she had ever saved in addition to her mother's life insurance was giving her some extra comfort in being able to take this extended trip.

Finally, after the second to last of the lines, she settled into a hard plastic chair and waited for her flight to board. Eventually, her row was called.

As patiently as she could, Everleigh walked over to stand in the long, slow line as other travelers meandered down the Jetway. She smiled, thinking they looked like lethargic lemmings on the way to the cliff's edge, every one of them hurrying up just so they could wait again.

She had been careful to book a window seat so she wouldn't miss anything. Having never flown, Everleigh was more interested in experiencing the flight than in the people around her, though every part of traveling was fascinating and fun for her.

No one else in her row had boarded yet, so it made getting settled less rushed. She pulled out the bag of goodies she had bought in the airport and a book out of the side pockets of her carry-on; then she placed it in the overhead compartment. She then slid across the seats, sat down, and buckled up. She wasn't thinking about the actual flight. She felt like she was bracing herself, not just physically but emotionally as well.

She heard Bette Davis in her head. "Buckle up; it's going to be a bumpy night."

"Good afternoon and welcome aboard Flight 527 to Dublin," a calming voice said over the speakers.

Everleigh couldn't see who was talking, but the woman's voice sounded lovely, with a slight accent she could not place that made her feel as if she had already left Seattle. The voice went on speaking about storing luggage, safety protocols, emergency exits, and that they would soon be on their way.

Everleigh's seatmate, a man wearing a suit that looked like it had been worn for a few days, showed up and sat in the aisle seat. No one was in the seat between them. Looking as worn-out as his suit, the wrinkled businessman placed a briefcase underneath the seat in front of him and laid back.

He's clearly done this before.

After what seemed an eternity, the engines revved up and the plane started to move, made its way down the runway, and gained speed. Everleigh leaned forward to watch as the ground rolled away beneath them, and she giggled a little as the jumbling of the plane made her stomach drop, not at all dissimilar to being on a rollercoaster. As they spent thirteen-plus hours soaring above North America and the Atlantic Ocean, Everleigh dozed a few times, waking up and nodding off. Her last nap provided a bit deeper sleep, the kind where you wake up and aren't quite sure what day it is. Soon after, the flight attendant passed out cards for going through customs. Everleigh quickly filled hers out, and then she watched the landing through the window, then a lengthy taxi to the gate, and then another long wait to get off the plane.

Everleigh was relieved she could just follow the crowd all along the way to passport control, and before long she stepped up to the border control agent.

"Passport and landing card please," the gentleman asked in a distinct Irish accent.

Everleigh handed over her documents.

"How long are you staying?"

"Six months."

"Are you here for business or pleasure?"

"Pleasure."

"Will you be staying in Ireland for the duration of your stay?"

"No, I'll be traveling throughout Europe."

"Where are you planning to travel?"

"Here...of course," Everleigh stuttered as she tried to get her thoughts in order. She hadn't expected to have to review her itinerary so immediately. "Scotland, France, Spain, and Greece. Maybe some other stops along the way."

"Have you been to Europe before?"

"This is my first trip here. First trip...anywhere."

"Well, it's about time. We've been waiting for you!"

Everleigh saw the huge smile on the agent's face, and she smiled back.

What a lovely welcome. This is meant to be.

The agent took a cursory look at her hotel confirmation, glanced again at her passport, stamped it, and handed it back to her. Everleigh could feel her heart rate drop. She'd made it!

"Enjoy your trip!"

"Thank you."

After making it out to the streets and onto the train, Everleigh was feeling invigorated. As the conductor sped off through the streets of Dublin, she watched through the window as buildings, street signs, vendors, and vehicles whizzed by. Everything around her seemed to have a more historical, more important feel than the surroundings at home.

Soon Everleigh had arrived at her hotel and checked in. She had chosen for her first night abroad to stay at Clontarf Castle Hotel. She liked its look and history, but also that it had an en suite bathroom, which she knew she wouldn't have once she started staying in hostels. She wanted to stay at a hotel her first few nights in Europe where she could see and feel the history, and this seemed like the place. She had read about the hotel in the travel brochures:

> *Clontarf Castle (Irish: Caisleán Chluain Tarbh) is a much-modernized castle. It is famous in the area as a key location of the Battle of Clontarf in 1014 with a castle on the site since 1172. Rebuilt in 1873, the castle in modern times functions as a hotel, bar, cabaret, and wedding venue...*

Everleigh wasn't ready to share facilities with strangers just yet since she planned to stay in hostels for most of her trip, but not her first night in Ireland. After checking in and dropping off her things in the room, her first order of business was finding something to eat. She was voracious by the time she arrived in her room, and she felt intense hunger pangs as she fantasized about the food in her near future.

"Excuse me," she said to the woman at the front desk.

"Yes, ma'am?" the woman asked. She looked tired, the cost of being in the service industry where everybody's needs matter but your own.

"I was hoping you could tell me where I can find a place to get some dinner. I'd like to walk if I can, so something nearby."

"Of course. There are a lot of places to eat just a few blocks away. If you walk out the front doors and turn left, up that road you'll see the pubs. There's Italian food, seafood, Pakistani; we even have a McDonald's if you're wanting American food."

"Is it obvious that I'm an American?"

"Quite! The accent."

"Oh, right."

"Enjoy your evening. If you would like any more recommendations for the duration of your stay, I'm here to help."

"I have a few places in mind but would love some tips. Thank you."

"Come find me. I'm here till 10 p.m. every night. My name is Sandra."

"Thank you, Sandra, and thanks for the directions."

"Of course."

Everleigh meandered out onto the streets of Dublin, finding herself surprised at how different it looked compared to what she had expected. Every picture that she had viewed online was of lush greenery, old stone buildings, and rolling hills. It was like that except dirtier, much less pristine. The sky was a deep, dark blue, the kind you see only in certain areas of America. Walking in the cool, misty evening air was surreal as she tried to take in every inch of scenery around her.

Everleigh was so hungry that the specific food didn't matter to her now, so she figured she would walk until the first pub she saw that looked interesting and stop there. A mile or so up the road, she landed on a traditional, yet upscale Irish pub that had a menu of classic Irish fare with modern takes. She felt like she could order one of everything on the menu and eat it all, but she remembered that she had her daily budget, so she ordered more modestly than her appetite.

A soup of the day with soda bread to start with, then the crispy fried Tipperary brie coated in panko breadcrumbs, served with baby mixed leaves, and a rich spiced berry compote. Truly, it was one of the best meals Everleigh had ever experienced. Satisfied and full after every bite, she went back to her hotel.

As Everleigh entered, Sandra was still at the front desk, but on the phone. She gave Everleigh a polite nod, and Everleigh returned a slight wave as she headed to her room. She changed out of the clothes she had been wearing since she left Seattle. It felt so good to pull on the comfortable sweats she had brought for sleeping and crawl into the massive bed in the middle of the room.

The blankets were heavy and warm, weighing her into a deep, comforting sleep.

The light coming in through the window woke Everleigh the next morning, and as she began to stretch, she remembered she had been so jetlagged that she had fallen asleep without closing the curtains the night before. With so many emotions running through her, she tried to get her bearings for a moment. She felt somewhat nervous realizing she was in Europe all on her own; she was also extremely excited. She imagined her grandmother had perhaps felt similarly, wondering about all that the future would bring on this journey of hers. After a long and much-needed shower, Everleigh put her hair in a ponytail and threw on jeans, walking shoes, a shirt, and a sweater. *The quintessential tourist attire!*

Grabbing her camera and her grandmother's well-used travel book, she walked downstairs to the complimentary breakfast. On the way, she thought about all she wanted to see, like some of the places her grandmother had stayed and visiting museums nearby, but beyond that, she just wanted to explore. As she entered the lobby, she saw Sandra again.

She must never leave, she thought.

"Good morning. Are you ready to head out for the day?" Sandra asked.

"Yes, I have a couple of places in mind to start with."

"What's number one on your list?"

"In the '50s, my grandmother traveled all over Europe by herself, so, I'm going to retrace her trip."

"That sounds brilliant, I've got a map you can take with you."

Sandra pulled out an easy-fold map and circled a few places she thought Everleigh might like to visit.

"Oh, this is very helpful. Thank you!" Everleigh said.

Everleigh showed Sandra one of the photos of Grandma Susan, standing in Dublin with her trusty bike next to her.

"That's perfect!" Sandra exclaimed, looking at the photo.

Everleigh always felt eager to talk about this aspect of her trip with others because they always seemed almost as excited as she was, and there was something very gratifying about sharing it. Sandra told Everleigh where she could rent a bicycle for the day, and Everleigh made notes.

"It looks like good weather for sightseeing; you have a wonderful day now," Sandra said.

"I hope so; thank you!" Everleigh replied as she left.

Simply getting to Europe had been such an accomplishment, and Everleigh felt ready to take on the world as she cycled around the streets of Dublin. There was much to see, to do, to be, to eat, to explore, to take photos of, and to experience.

It was an entirely new world opening up for her, and being in it, Everleigh felt invigorated, as if she could totally leave her small world behind and expand into soaring new heights. Here she was, realizing an actual dream. She became so entranced in her own thoughts and deep exploration and cycling through Dublin that it was quite a few hours before she realized she was completely lost.

CHAPTER 7

Everleigh wasn't sure where she was or how to get back to her hotel. She wasn't even on a main road. She must have been out and about for hours since dusk was now setting in. She felt a quick sense of panic wash over; she had the map Sandra had given her earlier in the day, but it wouldn't be much help because she had gone off the main roads.

She had spent much of her time cycling around exactly as she had imagined doing. She had been so enthralled by her surroundings that she had just wandered sans destination. There were so many items on her to-do list, from Grandma Susan's trip to her own desired destinations, yet she hadn't seemed to accomplish much of any of it today.

Everleigh knew she had time and that was okay, but snapping back into reality was jarring. She knew she would have to start figuring out her way back to her temporary home. Just when Everleigh became overwhelmed with the thought of being lost in a place she had never been before, she heard a friendly voice behind her.

"Do you need some help?" a woman asked.

Everleigh turned around to see another cyclist, who had seemingly come out of nowhere.

She looked around, wondering where this woman could have possibly come from. She seemed to have appeared out of thin air just in the nick of time to save Everleigh's day. Not feeling hesitant at all and trusting another young female cyclist, Everleigh nodded her head.

"Yes, thank you very much. I'm lost as lost can be. I need to find my way back to my hotel before the sun sets."

The cyclist was clearly a local. The accent was a dead giveaway. "Whereabouts are you staying?"

"I'm at the Clontarf."

"All right, follow me then, and I will get you back onto the main road."

In a few moments, they were well on their way and soon the cyclist had led Everleigh back into a recognizable spot. Everleigh felt a great appreciation for this friendly stranger and mused that she could be an angel. She also felt proud of herself for accepting the help of a kind person, something she was never too keen on doing.

Now in a place she was familiar with, Everleigh stopped to thank the cyclist, but she was nowhere to be found.

The next morning, Everleigh was ready and raring to get back out onto the streets of Ireland and continue exploring. Everleigh loved how she had been waking up feeling invigorated these past few days. Her excitement had not wavered much, only a little here and there, especially when she found herself lost, or when she let reality hit her for too long and she felt the fear of traveling alone as a young woman.

CHAPTER 8

Everleigh pored over the pages about Dublin from Grandma Susan touring around the city with her friend, Anton. She seemed to have met him where she was staying, at one of the hostels that had been rebuilt after World War II, but from what Everleigh could find, it didn't exist anymore. She read a few more pages:

I wanted to make sure my money lasted as long as my trip, so I cancelled the hotel and found a quaint hostel in the area. I was already on an adventure, so staying in a place most of the people I knew would call "Bohemian" seemed a grand idea. I will only admit it in these pages, but I was a bit nervous about the dormitory setting they offered. Sleeping in a room with strangers is *not* something I am used to doing. I was glad to know they separated the girls' rooms from the boys' rooms. Just imagine the scandal a co-ed sleeping arrangement would cause if they found out back home! Yesterday, I met Anton, a young man just out of school. He's here getting things set up for his wedding—can you believe that? A man making all the arrangements. His fiancée is completing school and will join him here. He's invited me to spend some time sightseeing, and I'm thrilled.

I have no idea what to see, but Anton knows the area well. He's fascinated with churches and wants to show me where he and Maria will be married. Imagine two Italians being married in Dublin! Well, I'm off for now to see the sights. The churches await.

Everleigh was so impressed with her grandmother's independence and spirit for adventure. That was something they had in common. Everleigh had always wondered where she had gotten it from, and now she knew. The churches her grandmother had listed included Christ Church Cathedral, St. Patrick's Cathedral, St. Audoen's Church, and John's Lane Church. She decided to make her way to all of them, and she would start with John's Lane.

John's Lane was the farthest away, but it made sense to start there to be sure she could see them all. It was walkable, but Everleigh thought cycling would be the best way to really take everything in as she moved around. The day was beautiful; a few rays of sun streamed in through a mostly overcast sky, and by the time she reached John's Lane Church, Everleigh was finally warming up. She took off her hoodie and shoved it into her backpack; then she pulled out her camera and the photo. She quickly found the spot where Grandma Susan and Anton had posed for their picture.

Everleigh snapped a few quick shots and then stood, staring at the brown and red stonework. While leaning on the stone wall in front of her, she recognized the same pattern, the exact stone her grandmother had traced in her journal. Everleigh placed her hand in the same spot and sensed an energy that had been left so many years before. Perhaps, it was all in her head, but she truly felt connected to this woman she had never known.

We have a very similar spirit, Everleigh thought.

"Can I take a picture of you?" a voice asked.

"What?" Everleigh asked as she was pulled back to reality.

"Would you like for me to take a picture of you by the church?" asked a young woman. She was as much a tourist as Everleigh, with her own backpack and camera.

"Would you mind? Can you take it from the same angle as this photo?" Everleigh asked, handing her the old black and white of "Susan and Anton" along with her camera.

"No problem. This is a great picture. Who are the people in it?"

"The woman is my grandmother, Susan."

"Is that your grandfather?"

"No, he was a friend she met when she traveled here in the '50s. In fact, he and his fiancée were married in this very church."

"That's a great story! Okay, back up a bit and move to the left. I mean your right, my left. Let's see how close we can make this match. Tilt your head a bit and smile. Perfect!"

The woman clicked away, clearly enjoying herself. Everleigh was enjoying herself as well.

"Thank you so much. By the way, my name is Everleigh."

"Oh, I'm Kim. You're American, too?" she asked.

"Yes, from Seattle. What about you?" Everleigh asked.

"I'm from California. Getting ready to start college soon, so I decided to travel a bit first. I guess that whole rite of passage into adulthood, you know?"

"I do. I'm doing mine a bit late, but better late than never."

"Totally! How long have you been in Dublin?"

"A few days. This is my first day really sightseeing, though."

"I got in two days ago. My friends are all sleeping in. Too much fun at the pubs last night! I was bored waiting for them to get up, so I headed out. I'm fascinated with these old churches."

"Me too. I've got at least three others I want to see today."

"Would you mind some company? We could be each other's photographers. My friends laugh at me for being such a 'real tourist.' Taking photos everywhere and of everything."

"I would love the company."

"Let's go inside," Kim said, nodding toward the church, and with that, they entered John's Lane Church and gasped at the sight of the stained-glass windows and innate fixtures that sprawled throughout. They took pictures and pointed out interesting things to each other. The duo trekked to all the churches on Everleigh's list and found a few more along the way. By the time they stopped for a bite to eat, it was late afternoon. They both ordered salads at an outdoor eatery and sipped on dark, creamy stouts. Everleigh sat back and felt the sun on her face.

"My friends will be up and ready to go by now. I can't wait to tell them I met the coolest chick from Seattle and that we've been playing tourist all day! Let's take a photo of the two of us!" Kim said, jumping up to come around behind Everleigh. She knelt next to her so they would be sitting head-to-head and snapped a quick shot.

"Oh, that's going to be great; I just know it!" Kim said. "They'll want me to come back and get into trouble with them for a bit. Will you meet us later at a pub? I want you to meet them all and have some beers with us."

"That sounds fun. Which pub?"

"Hmm...something Irish," she said and laughed at how silly that sounded. "How about "O'Donoghue's? They've got killer Irish music and it's so much fun. There's another place that has cheap drinks that we may hit later, but we'll start at O'Donoghue's for sure. Meet us there at about eight o'clock?"

"Okay, I'll be there."

"Great. I'll look for you. I'd better go before they get all fussy. Thanks for letting me hang with you today. I had a blast!"

"Me too. See you later!"

Kim ran off to meet up with her friends. After all the walking and beer, Everleigh sank farther into her chair, taking in the cool air before walking back to the hotel. After returning to her temporary home, she kicked off her shoes and laid down to take a nap.

It didn't take long for Everleigh to drift off to sleep. After an hour of napping, she stirred and decided she would get ready for the pub. She gathered up her bath supplies and took a lengthy, refreshing shower. After slipping into some clean jeans, a T-shirt, and a jacket, she headed out to O'Donoghue's where she would meet her new friend Kim and hopefully make a few more. The pub was easy to find, but Kim was nowhere to be seen. The music was just getting started, and Kim had been right about the band; it was great traditional Irish music.

Everleigh walked to the bar and ordered another dark, draft beer, Guinness, which is the common beer of Ireland.

After receiving her drink, she sat at a small corner table as close to the band as she could find. Even if Kim and her friends didn't show, she would still have a good time, though she was hoping they hadn't changed their minds. Everleigh didn't mind being alone too much; hell, she'd spent most of her life alone. Though she enjoyed solitude, she was finding it easy to meet new people and make friends. She was beginning to feel odd in the moments when she found herself alone. There were too many pressing things she would need to think about and sort through, but she didn't want to focus on them just yet. About forty-five minutes and a few draft beers later, Everleigh heard Kim screaming her name over the crowd and music.

"Everleigh! There you are! Come over here; we found a big table for all of us."

Kim came up to her table and gave her a big long-lost friend kind of hug. She grabbed Everleigh's hand and pulled her through the room. She stopped at a table with four beautiful, young people.

"Everleigh, this is my gang of weirdos! The blond guy is Kevin, and that's Tiffany, Robert, and Laurie. Everyone, this is Everleigh!" Everyone smiled and held up a beer to cheer the new friendship.

After the usual pleasantries, Robert offered Everleigh a chair, and Kevin went off to the bar to order more beer. The mood was festive, and the band was loud. Everyone was talking at the same time and laughing at their own jokes. Everleigh laughed along with them all, but she mostly observed. She didn't know their inside jokes, but she could tell they were good people, and she felt safe with them. Soon they were all up and dancing, working up a sweat and drinking more beer. Then the time came to head off to the other pubs. Not wanting to miss a moment with them, and knowing she would be moving on to the next leg of her journey in the coming days, Everleigh followed along willingly.

CHAPTER 9

The next leg of Everleigh's journey would include her staying in hostels for the first time ever, something she was very much looking forward to. Everleigh packed up her things and checked out of the beautiful Clontarf Castle. She was feeling happy, but something was nagging her in the pit of her stomach; somehow, it also tickled a far-back place in her mind where she stashed certain things away for another day. She'd had so much fun the night before and made so many beautiful new friends that she didn't like these feelings fighting their way in, trying to drag her down. Everything continued to feel bittersweet for her.

Had she really believed she could run away from the details of her life, the reality of all she'd just learned? Death was something she hadn't thought about much at all. Now, she was misplacing her annoyance with her inability to cope with reality. Along with this lightbulb of an idea, all the grief hit her in an undeniable rush.

Tears filled Everleigh's eyes, but she did her best not to let them fall as she looked over at the bicycle she had rented. Cycling had usually brought her a lot of joy or at least comfort. She'd much rather bike around Seattle than drive a car or take a bus.

She was grieving the loss of her mother, yes, but added to that was the newfound grief of a life lost, of years not really knowing who she was and why her relationship with her mother had been so strained. She felt angry too.

She had been cheated out of a lot of normal things she should have experienced. Among these feelings was also the question of whether her brother had fared any better by being adopted. So many questions. She didn't like thinking of such ugly things. She tried to remind herself in these terrible moments that she had promised herself to stay present and enjoy this trip. She didn't want to look back at this trip and regret that she had spent it being sad.

Instead, she thought about her plans for the immediate future. She could deal with the grief, the intrusive thoughts, and anything else later. There would be plenty of time for all of that, and there would be plenty of time to grieve. Forever, in fact. For now, she would leave Dublin behind and make her way to Belfast and on.

She could take a train from Dublin to Belfast—it would only take a little over three hours. Everleigh loved trains; she loved that they felt old-fashioned, and she could pretend she was in another era as she watched the scenery speed by. There was something truly romantic about trains. They created pleasant thoughts she could easily shift her attention to.

Everleigh bid a sweet goodbye to Sandra, one of the first friendly faces in Europe she had met and headed on her way. She was hoping to make it quickly to the train station so she could set everything down, relax, and enjoy the ride. She wasn't too sure of her plans once she arrived in Belfast other than finding a hostel to stay in.

The three-hour train ride was pleasant, and before Everleigh knew it, she had arrived in Belfast. Once Everleigh disembarked the train and was on the platform, she opened the map to get her bearings. A voice behind her asked, "Can I help you find something?" Everleigh turned to see a woman, well-aged and eager to help.

"My name is Glenna, Glenna Higgins, used to be O'Higgins, but the 'O' got dropped way back. Anyway, I'm Glenna. Dear, can I help you find something? I know the area quite well."

Taken aback by the woman's openness, Everleigh said, "I'll be staying here for a few days and need to find a hostel."

Glenna was quick to answer. "I know of just the place, and it's close enough to the nearby sights. You'll just love it!"

With all the pleasantries Everleigh had forgotten to introduce herself; "Sorry; I'm Everleigh, Everleigh Ford. How long have you lived here, Glenna?"

"Born and raised. I went away to school for a bit but came back and did the usual. Got married and settled down, had two children, but they've moved off, so I only see them when they're on holiday."

Sensing a loneliness and deep longing for companionship in Glenna, Everleigh, without thinking, blurted out, "Would you like some company today?"

Glenna, without hesitation, replied, "Sure, that would be wonderful, dear!"

Everleigh was finding it very easy to make new friends.

"Glenna, I have a great idea. Have you eaten? Are you hungry?"

"No, I haven't, and yes, I am," Glenna replied with her sweet smile.

"How about you and I go out for dinner?" said Everleigh.

"Really?" Glenna was clearly thrilled by the idea. Everleigh wasn't sure if it was the food or the company that made her so happy. "Sounds lovely."

Either way, Everleigh realized she, too, was looking forward to sharing a meal with somebody. She had been eating alone since yesterday, so the company would be good for her. Glenna was a delight, and she probably had a list of places for Everleigh to visit. She'd know if any of the places her Grandma Susan had mentioned were still around. It was a win-win for them both.

"Where to?" Everleigh asked as they headed on.

Once they had made it to the restaurant of Glenna's choosing, which was cozy and quaint, with lots of wood and brick and low lighting, Everleigh felt herself relax and ease into a gentle conversation with this kind stranger, her new friend. Every corner of the restaurant seemed to be a nook for sitting, reading, and visiting. Everleigh was enchanted.

Glenna sat down on one of the couches, staring off into the mid-distance. Everleigh noticed how small and frail she seemed, and a lump caught in her throat as she thought of her mother. It was the first time she'd really thought about her mother in this way. There was suddenly a flurry of emotions from grief and sadness to anger and denial. Everleigh wasn't ready to deal with any of these emotions; she shook her head as if to shake off the thoughts. She knew she had a lot of processing to do, but now was not the time. As she settled into a nearby comfy chair, she reflected on her dinner with Glenna.

Their conversation was pleasant, and Everleigh enjoyed Glenna's wry sense of humor. It was the kind of easy joking that alluded to a life well-lived and having "seen it all" but having the good sense not to mention the details.

That's something that must come with age, Everleigh thought.

Everleigh hoped someday she would have a memory of full experiences that would afford her that little glint in the eye that Glenna wore so easily. That was a distant dream, but a dream nonetheless, and Everleigh was becoming more set on actualizing her dreams than ever before. Dusk was setting in and it was time to call it a day. Glenna and Everleigh walked a short distance to the hostel Glenna suggested. Everleigh felt bittersweet leaving Glenna because of how much she reminded her of her mother and how easily they had become friends. A moment of grief welled up in her, realizing that she could never again attempt to get to know her own mother.

After exchanging contact information, so Everleigh could send a postcard, and a warm embrace, Everleigh walked into the hostel and up to the desk.

"Do you have any beds for tonight?"

"We sure do," said the female clerk. "Are you okay with co-ed, or do you need a women's room?"

Everleigh immediately thought of Grandma Susan and smiled. She wasn't so worried about the scandal, but she knew she wanted to feel comfortable. She looked up at the young woman and stifled a giggle. She looked like a guest herself and she probably was. Everleigh had read that some people stay for extended periods and get discounted rates by working the front lobby and helping check in other guests.

"A women's room, please," Everleigh said, knowing her grandmother would approve.

"We've got a ten-bed or a six-bed."

"I'll take the six-bed, thanks."

"No problem. I need you to fill this out," said the clerk, handing her a guest card.

"Is there any problem if I decide to stay longer than one night?" asked Everleigh.

"We just need to know in the morning to keep your bed from getting booked."

"Okay, great."

Everleigh showed her passport and paid for the room in cash. She'd need to get to a bank to get more since she'd spent it faster than she expected. She would ask about a bank later, but for now, she wanted to throw her bags in a locker and check out the laundry facilities; she *really* needed to wash some things. *That's the downside to traveling light; you don't have a lot of clean clothes,* she thought. As she made her way to the room, she was thrilled that she'd stepped up to the dorm room challenge.

She found her room easily enough and could see from suitcases and other items piled on the other beds that she had the last unclaimed bed. It would be a full house.

CHAPTER 10

Eleven o'clock came fast the next day. It was much later than Everleigh would normally get up, but she was so exhausted from traveling and getting settled into her new hostel that she slept hard. She took a hot shower, put on comfortable clothes, and got coffee—she needed loads of coffee to get her up and moving today. She hadn't bought any groceries, but the hostel provided a few things for breakfast, so she grabbed a bagel from the community kitchen and toasted it. As she sat down to eat, a few of the other guests greeted her. She smiled politely but was trying to plan out her day, eager to view the peace walls.

In her guidebook, Everleigh had read how Northern Ireland was scarred by lethal sectarian violence known as "The Troubles." This volatile era was fraught with riots, car bombings, police brutality, civil disobedience, and revenge killings that ran from the late 1960s until the present day. The Troubles were seeded by centuries of conflict between predominantly Catholic Ireland and predominantly Protestant England. After conflicts erupted into violence in the late 1960s, leaving over 3,600 dead, and more than 30,000 injured, no-go areas were created to segregate hostile parties, which is why the peace walls were built in some sectors, allowing people to find temporary reprieve in their respective areas.

Everleigh was feeling some mixture of emotions as she left the hostel. She was surprised to encounter tanks rolling down the street. Behind them were three green army Jeeps with soldiers standing behind machine guns on turrets pointed at the countryside. Following the tanks were two trucks, each with men heavily armed and weapons drawn. Everleigh felt a wash of nerves rush over her, questioning her safety. She knew there had been unrest in Belfast, but seeing it in person was much different from hearing or reading about it. With the tanks in full sight rolling down the highway, there was no doubt things were different here. She decided to busy herself with the pamphlet she found on the hostel bulletin board. It told her all about the peace walls and the area's history.

Every place had its own issues and almost every group of people had some history of hating another group. But the Catholic/Protestant tension was unique. Both groups were Christian, yet it was more than religion that separated them.

Everleigh's grandmother had been in Belfast in 1953, before "The Troubles" started, but even then, there was some tension between the Catholics and Protestants. It was more a time of tolerance and peace back then, but just a few short years later, the peace lines or peace walls started to go up in hopes of protecting lives.

Everleigh read that the walls separated neighborhoods, and some ran right down the middle of a city street separating one side from another.

Even though the walls were very tall, the opposing side still managed to lob Molotov cocktails over them and cause injuries to unsuspecting "neighbors" on the opposite side. Everleigh knew some of the walls were already down and she had read that there was talk of removing all of them in the future.

Everleigh rarely strayed off the straight and narrow, but something about this felt right, purposeful. Besides, the clerk who checked her in had assured her it was very safe; tourists went to see the walls all the time. She discovered just one taxi on the street. The driver rolled down the window as she walked up. The whole thing felt a bit "cloak and dagger."

"Need a ride, do you?" the driver asked.

"I do. Is it possible for you to take me to the peace walls?" Everleigh asked.

"Yes, of course! I take people there every day," he replied. "My name is Rodney, and I am at your service. I'll take you on the grand tour of the peace walls."

Rodney had so easily agreed that Everleigh felt quite at ease getting into the cab. She barely had the door closed before he took off into the busy streets. She began taking a few pictures out of the window, but she knew they would likely not turn out too well because Rodney was zipping this way and that. In fact, Everleigh double-checked her seatbelt more than once. They turned a corner and were in a normal-looking neighborhood, and then a larger road headed toward the northwest sections of Belfast. There were signs of destruction everywhere; it truly looked like a war zone.

"I know these streets and will only stop where it's safe," Rodney said. "There are some places I won't stop, but we'll speed through the rough patches."

Then Everleigh saw them. A long line of barrier walls, separating one side of the community from another. They were tall and intimidating with steel sections and wire sections above that. They were about twenty-five feet tall, and Everleigh had to lean her head out of the car window to take in how massive they were. What amazed her was all the graffiti and art painted on the lower sections. Most were messages of hope and peace, and the colors were amazingly bright and cheerful on what would otherwise be a drab dull blight along the road. These murals were painted on the sides of apartment buildings, garages, and city walls. Rodney explained that some of the murals held messages for rival gangs and were ways for the gangs to communicate with each other.

Rodney suddenly pulled over and told her it would be fine to get out there to take some photos. Everleigh started with a few long shots, trying to capture the immensity of what she saw. Then she focused on the murals. She thought it was some of the most hopeful and sad artwork she had ever seen. She noticed that Rodney had lit a cigarette and was sitting there, not really paying any attention. Everleigh felt safe enough and walked down the road toward an open gate.

It was painted with the most colorful mural of freedom leaders, quotes, and images. To get a good picture, Everleigh had to walk through the gate a bit onto the other side. She was focusing on her pictures, not paying attention to her surroundings, when she heard some voices up the street.

Everleigh turned to see three young men heading down the street in her direction.

Chances were they would offer no trouble, but rather than push her luck, she decided she had enough photos, headed back to the cab, and jumped inside.

"You got enough pictures?" Rodney asked, already pulling away from the curb.

"Yes, thank you. It's amazing to see all this," Everleigh replied.

Rodney nodded but didn't respond. He weaved his way down the streets and back toward the spot where she'd found him, near the hostel. As the cab drove by a roadside barricade, Everleigh quickly snapped a photo of the police standing guard at the enclosure.

"That's not a good idea," Rodney said. "Taking photos of the police is not something you do here. They could pull us over and ask for your camera."

"Really? Would they take my camera from me?"

"They might, that or the roll of film. They don't like pictures being taken."

"Will you get into any trouble?"

"Me? No. Don't worry about that."

Everleigh held her breath and glanced a few times out the back window, searching for police lights and wondering if she was about to hear sirens. After five minutes, she looked down at her camera and breathed a sigh of relief. Nothing had happened.

"Looks like you're a lucky one!" Rodney said. "If they were going to pull us over, they would have done it."

"Are you sure?" Everleigh asked.

"Yes. It doesn't take them this long to make a stop. You're in the clear."

"And I have a rare photo, it seems."

"That you do. One for framing."

"Yes, one for framing. Thank you, Rodney."

They sat in silence for the remainder of the car ride until Rodney pulled up to the curb where Everleigh had found him. She paid her fare and gave a generous tip; Rodney deserved it.

When Everleigh returned to the hostel, she secured her camera in her locker, grabbed her dirty clothes, and walked down the hall to the laundry room. After folding her clothes, she wandered downstairs to fix a cup of tea. She lay back in her bunk that night, musing about seeing the peace walls, reminiscing about what she had discovered in Belfast.

A few hours later, Everleigh was awakened by the others in the room stumbling in drunk, loud, and trying to be quiet. Everleigh pretended to be asleep, and after about twenty minutes, things were quiet again because her fellow tourists had all passed out. She hoped she didn't snore as loudly as the girl in the bed next to hers.

Everleigh rose early the next morning and headed out for a proper breakfast. A few of her roommates were stirring, but slowly. Hangovers were clearly an international experience. She invited one of the more alert travelers to join her, but she declined, having to wait for her friend who was still asleep. Everleigh grabbed Grandma Susan's travel journal and headed out. She found a wonderful place to enjoy a large, hearty, and nourishing breakfast. She thumbed through the journal and noted that her grandmother had commented on several churches in Belfast:

> Anton has inspired me. Now I'm making a point to see as many old churches as I can. Here in Belfast, the list includes Belfast Cathedral (or St. Anne's as the locals call it), St. Patrick's Catholic, May Street Presbyterian, and First Presbyterian—one of the oldest places of worship with a history going back to 1783.

After eating all she could, Everleigh walked to both St. Anne's and First Presbyterian churches. She felt a deep satisfaction knowing she was sharing a view and maybe even standing in the same spots her grandmother had stood decades earlier. She took in the local sights, pawed through some tourist shops, and grabbed some things to take back to the hostel for dinner. It had been a lovely, quiet day to regain her energy and think about her grandmother and her next destination, Galway.

The next day, Everleigh was on her way to Galway, a harbor city on Ireland's west coast at the mouth of where the River Corrib meets the Atlantic Ocean.

As the train entered Galway, Everleigh could see that nearby there were stone-clad cafes, boutiques, and art galleries lining winding lanes between sections of some medieval city walls that were still standing. As she spent more time in Europe, Everleigh was continually struck by how old and historical everything around her was. Seattle had its perks, and she loved home, but this was simply different. It felt so big, so important. There was so much history; she wondered if the other tourists who came through these parts had the same thoughts.

Everleigh often wondered if she and her grandmother had very similar moments and thoughts on their trips nearly forty years apart. She liked to think they did.

Stepping off the train, Everleigh looked at the picturesque beauty that was Galway. She remembered reading that it dated back to the medieval era; even more breathtaking was that it was a harbor city, large and charming. It was one of Ireland's most populated cities so she just knew there would be nightlife and beautiful traditional Irish music to be heard.

She would need to find a hostel and relieve herself of her baggage. She arrived in Eyre Square, and directly off the train, there were hostels, so she walked through the square, keeping her eyes open for her next housing. Just a few minutes of cruising later, Everleigh happened upon Kinlay Hostel; it was exactly what she needed, affordable and tidy.

She checked in, taking a room she would share with three travelers. She dropped her luggage off and rented a bicycle that she would ride back into the streets after freshening up.

Everleigh wasn't exactly certain what she wanted to see in Galway, but she knew she would at least spend a day or two wandering the city and perhaps finding some nightlife. She had never been much of a partier, but she was here, and she was determined to live it up, at least a little, or at least her version of living it up—like she had done a couple of nights ago, making friends, taking pictures, creating memories. *That* was exactly the intention Everleigh had set for the trip even when it was just a simple idea.

Eyre Square was a lush, vibrant meeting place right in the city center of Galway. Everleigh thought to take her bike and sit in the shade beneath one of the many ash trees and watch the hubbub of the city for a while. The air smelled sweet and green, with a tinge of moisture in it. Spring in Ireland felt just like fall in Seattle. She leaned her bike against one of the park's massive trees and sat down, looking out onto the park and the city square. Suddenly, she heard a commotion of distant beating drums. Then, louder, and louder. She looked around, trying to ascertain where the clamor was coming from and what exactly it was.

Then, even louder, more drums and more people just about a hundred feet away from her. She hopped back on her bicycle and headed over.

Wow! It's...a drum circle.

Formed out of seemingly nothing and nowhere. Everleigh stood watching as a group of men and women played on and other passersby stopped to watch. What was so mesmerizing about the drum circle was that it offered equality because there was no beginning or end; it seemed to include everyone—people of all ages, sexes, and backgrounds—sitting and sharing rhythm with each other.

After watching the drum circle for more time than she realized, Everleigh thought about how this was a very interesting and unique way of forming a group consciousness.

This is really something!

Everleigh watched for a long time, and when she finally returned to her hostel, she noticed a group of people playing pool in the lobby. They looked like they were having a good time, and she stopped to watch the game for a bit. Observing people here was almost as fun as experiencing things for herself.

"Fancy a game?" a voice broke through Everleigh's trance.

"Excuse me?" Everleigh said, looking up at a young man about her age. He had tousled red hair and a big smile to go with his bright green eyes.

"Fancy a game? Don't sit there watching us play. Why don't you join in?"

"Oh, I'm not very good," Everleigh said.

"Damn, I was hoping you were a shark," he replied.

"Not even close."

"No worries," a blonde standing by their table said. "None of us are, even when we're sober. Come join us."

"All right!" Everleigh beamed, all too eager to make even more friends.

"My name's Tommy," the redhead said, extending his hand for a proper shake.

"I'm Everleigh," she replied and offered a firm, confident hand.

"I'm Ruth," the blonde said and added, "This is Liam," referring to a dark-haired man with a beard.

"We're playing eight-ball," Liam said as he nodded toward Everleigh.

"I think that's the only game I know." Everleigh smiled. She felt comfortable since everyone at the table had warm, friendly smiles. Tommy racked the balls and Ruth broke. She sank a solid ball with the break and went on to line up another shot.

"We're stripes." Tommy smiled. "Let's hope we get a chance. Ruth's found pool to be her hidden talent." Ruth did sink another ball, but then missed her next shot.

"You jinxed me, Tommy!" she teased.

"All right, Everleigh, you're up!" Tommy stepped back and made room for Everleigh.

She grabbed the pool cue leaning against the wall and hoped she didn't completely embarrass herself.

The weight of the pool cue felt good in her hands, and she was grateful to see a striped ball lined up neatly with a corner pocket. After a deep breath, she leaned over to line up her shot. How long had it been since she had played pool?

That she couldn't easily recall confirmed that it had been an awfully long time. Everleigh slid the cue back and felt the smooth wood slide through her fingers that were perched on the table.

Here goes nothing, she thought.

A slight tap on the cue ball sent it across the table and toward the blue-striped ball.

Sink the ball. Please, please, please! Clunk. Successfully, the ball sank into the corner pocket.

"Brilliant!" Tommy shouted.

"Well done," Liam said.

"I thought you didn't play well," Ruth said. "Carry on, Everleigh. Carry on."

Everleigh just grinned with delight and made the next two shots before she was done. There really wasn't much of a shot left for her to take, so she acquiesced to the table with a sense of pride. Tommy, Ruth, and Liam were so much fun, and very soon, they were all laughing and kidding around as if she had been friends with them for years. She and Tommy won the first game but lost the next two. No one really seemed to care about winning or losing, though; it was just great to spend the evening this way. Her three pool mates were all from Ireland and attended the same school. They were just taking a quick break from their studies for some touring around the country. Tommy and Liam had been friends since childhood and Ruth had joined the gang as a "flatmate at university." That was how they said it, and the words felt comfortable on Everleigh's tongue as she repeated them. It amused her how the same language was spoken so many ways around the world.

"Thanks for joining us, Everleigh," Tommy said. "What are your plans for the rest of your stay here?"

"I'm not sure yet. My trip is a bit of an homage to my grandmother. I'm retracing as much of her trip as I can."

"Your Gran? When was she here?" Ruth asked.

"In the '50s. She traveled on her own, so I'm doing the same thing."

Liam said, looking straight at her, "Is this your first trip to Europe?"

"My first trip anywhere!"

"Well, if you travel like you play pool, you'll have no problems," Tommy said.

"Where else are you going?" Ruth asked.

"I'll visit Scotland, Belgium, Germany, Poland, France, Italy, Spain, and finally Greece."

"Wow! Did your Gran visit all those places?" Liam asked.

"Almost. She never made it to Spain or Greece, but they were on her list. I'm hoping to make it there for the both of us."

"I'm sure you'll do it," Ruth said.

"Why didn't she make it to Spain and Greece?" Tommy asked.

"She went back home to marry my grandfather. He got back from the war in Korea, so she went home to be with him."

"That is *so* romantic," Ruth said.

"It is, isn't it?" Everleigh replied; she had never looked at it that way herself.

The four of them chatted more before eventually saying goodnight. Everleigh asked if they'd be around in the morning, but Tommy said they had to get up early to head back home. Before they headed upstairs, Ruth insisted they take some pictures. She and Everleigh traded email addresses so Ruth could send the photos to her. They all hugged Everleigh and wished her luck on the rest of her travels. On the walk back to her room, Everleigh found her mind flooded with thoughts and worries she didn't realize she had packed along with her. She was so glad she'd said yes to playing pool. She'd had such a good time that she was genuinely sad she wouldn't see her new friends again.

As she drifted off to sleep for the night, her final thought was...

"Tomorrow, we head to Scotland, Grandma. We'll see what's changed!"

Everleigh spent the day relaxing, and sightseeing in town and caught an early evening ferry to Stranraer, Scotland. She was ready to check out Glasgow, the Isle of Skye, and Edinburgh. Those were the main places mentioned in her grandmother's journal that she had pulled out to read on the trip. What she hadn't expected were the rough waters on the ferry trip. She had imagined every ferry would be calm, breezy, and gorgeous. On this ride, huge swells scooped the ferry up and down, back and forth. A storm was headed in, and there was no stopping it or any signs of it slowing down.

Everleigh had planned on reading through her grandmother's journals of Scotland on the trip there, but the rough waters had abruptly put an end to those plans. It was all she could do to brace herself and keep her bottom attached to her seat. It was nighttime and very dark, so Everleigh couldn't see when the next large waves were coming and there was no way to brace for their impact. Travel was about the unexpected too, she had to remind herself. Maybe she would find her sea legs on this rocky ferry ride to Scotland.

Moments of exhaustion and slumber overcame Everleigh, only to be rudely interrupted by the unruly waters rocking the ferry. The nearly four-hour ride finally came to an end, taking much longer than normal because of the storm. Everleigh wobbled off the ship, hoping she could find a place to rest for a while before the bus tour of Glasgow she planned to take in the afternoon. There was a notice in the terminal for a small inn within walking distance, so Everleigh trudged toward it. Luckily, one small room was available.

The room was about the size of a walk-in closet and the bed was too soft and lumpy, but Everleigh didn't mind. She was happy to have a space to lie down, and she thought in comparison to the ferry ride, at least the room couldn't do any tossing and turning. Everleigh had a tough nap, waking up frequently with sore spots on her hips from the too-soft bed. She finally resigned herself to getting up, taking a sponge bath, throwing on some fresh clothes, and heading to the tour bus pick-up spot.

Near the bus stop, Everleigh found a small tea shop, so she bought herself some pastries to nibble and tea to sip. Strong black tea was in order as she watched for the bus through tired, squinty eyes. The bus was a double-decker, and despite being sleep-deprived, Everleigh felt excited as she climbed to the upper deck and took a seat. The tour did not disappoint, and it was nice to have someone pointing out exactly what things to notice. There were chances to hop off the bus and explore in more detail, though it was pleasant enough to sit back and enjoy the views. She snapped some photos as the driver pointed out some of the places her grandmother had mentioned in her journal:

Oh, there's some wonderful medieval buildings here in Glasgow, including Glasgow Cathedral (it survived the Reformation of 1560!). Then there's the City Chambers opened by Queen Victoria in 1888—they say it has more marble than the Vatican—imagine!

After the bus tour, Everleigh headed back to her hostel and her small, lumpy mattress. The combination of the rough ferry ride, a lack of sleep, and hunger gave Everleigh a raging headache.

She opened the window for some fresh air; a storm had hit, and it was now overcast and raining. The sweet, damp smell of rain filled the room within seconds as Everleigh lay down, taking it all in.

Everleigh loved the way the rain smelled, and even though her bed was small and not very comfortable, she was tired enough to find it all very soothing. She read through the journals and was in and out of sleep as the storm roared on. She spent the next few days taking in a few local sites, a few of which she'd seen on the tour and others that were mentioned in Grandma Susan's journal. She spent quite some time at Glasgow Cathedral, the birthplace of Glasgow. Stepping on floors her grandmother had walked and seeing those same stunning windows brought tears to Everleigh's eyes. All these experiences over the past few weeks and months were catching up to her and accumulating in her tear ducts.

It had been a lot—getting to know her grandmother on this trip, her mother's death, the funeral, the lawyer's office, the letter, her brother. She still wasn't sure about how she would deal with her "new" brother. She would have to start thinking about it all soon, sorting things out and deciding what she would do with her house now that it was hers and hers alone. She wandered the great aisles of Glasgow Cathedral, where she mused about all these things and more while she snapped photo after photo. Everleigh decided it was time to blow off some steam and meet some locals at another pub. Drinking and eating had quickly become one of Everleigh's favorite pastimes on this journey through Europe.

She found a stony, old-looking pub and slinked into a seat at one of the benches, ordering herself a lunch of fruit, cheese, nuts, bread, quince paste, and, of course, tea.

The barkeep poured her a glass of Drambuie once she was finished eating. It was a sweet, golden liqueur made from whiskey, herbs, spices, and heather honey. After taking a sip, the initial taste was overwhelmingly sweet and strong. Everleigh detected other notes, including honey, licorice, cinnamon, and orange zest.

Feeling warmed up from the inside out, Everleigh melted into the bench and thought about waiting there until the band would come and play. It wasn't like she had a strict itinerary to stick to while she was here. The freedom of being schedule-less was a wonderful feeling. Everleigh had always been a by-the-book sort of person. Though she was more adventurous than her mother had ever been, she had lived a relatively quiet life up until now. She had gone to school, graduated from high school, gotten a college degree, and been working the same office job ever since she had graduated. This really was her first taste, ever, of what it was like to follow her heart, live her dreams, and let her sense of adventure fly free—free of judgment from herself or others' expectations. She had been waiting her entire life to let her hair down like this. She even began eyeing all the cute men in the place, hoping to get a few free drinks.

When the band started, Everleigh was thrilled. All the band members were wearing kilts, and they played a mix of popular songs with a bagpipe accompaniment. She only recognized some of the songs, but she enjoyed all of it, pretending to know the ones she didn't.

In front of the band was a small dance floor, and many of the patrons made their way to it as the night carried on and spirits became jollier and more uninhibited.

This may have been the best night of her trip so far, and it got even better when the band started to play "You Can Leave Your Hat On" and the crowd went wild. At first, Everleigh thought it was just a crowd favorite, but soon she realized the band members were beginning to take off their clothes piece by piece as they played. They danced and stripped, just like in the movie, *The Full Monty!* It was hilarious, and everyone in the place *roared* with laughter and cheers, crowding the dance floor, shouting, and cat-calling the band as they carried on, loving every second of the attention their wild performance was getting. The place was very dim, which was great because Everleigh felt a little lascivious watching an entire band play completely in the nude, but they kept playing and it really didn't seem to faze them at all. Everleigh thought herself a little silly, feeling so sheepish; it was the '90s after all, and the times were very progressive; still, it was very unlikely to have happened at a bar anywhere in America.

CHAPTER 11

In the morning, Everleigh checked out of her hostel and continued her journey, which included the Isle of Skye. Everleigh was achingly ready for the next destination on her itinerary. She would be traveling a bit faster and spending less time in each place than her grandmother, but it satisfied her all the same. After touring through Loch Lomond and Glencoe (the site of the massacre of the MacDonald clan in 1692), she stopped for lunch in Fort William and started to discuss the area and things to do with fellow travelers. They mentioned that they had hiked Ben Nevis, which was stunning and close by. There was a hostel at the bottom of Ben Nevis, so you could just walk right out and hike in the morning, This sounded amazing to Everleigh, and since it was on the way to the Isle of Skye, she was going to do it.

Ben Nevis was considered the "Outdoor Capital of the UK." Glen Nevis Youth Hostel sat right at the foot of Ben Nevis with a path to the mountain leading directly from its door. Since Ben Nevis is Britain's highest mountain, at 4,413 feet above sea level, Everleigh was looking forward to the photo opportunities. The next day, after a good night's sleep, Everleigh was utterly determined to make the hike up Ben Nevis. The mountain was in Lochaber, about two miles from Fort William and part of the Nevis Range of Scotland's Grampian Mountains. With an average of only fourteen clear days a year on its summit, getting a good day on Ben Nevis would be great luck. She packed some food and water, put on her sturdy hiking boots, and set out for this adventure.

The climb would be eight or nine hours long, with the climb to the top being about four hours and the descent the same, or shorter, depending on the hiker's agility. Everleigh was fit from all the cycling she did, so she knew she could put herself to the task of climbing this grand mountain. She made quick progress, reaching the halfway point of the Red Burn and the Lochan Meall an t-Suidhe in a little over an hour. She just could not help stopping for pictures; the views across to Loch Linnhe, down to Lismore, and as far as the Isle of Mull were stunning. From the halfway point and on, she struggled a little more, but passing by other hikers also struggling to ascend gave her great encouragement. There was a well-made path, but it gave way to uneven boulders and slippery ground; the switchbacks seemed unending. She had read somewhere that the Ben was nicknamed "the venomous mountain," and now she understood why. The Mountain Track, also known as "the Ben Nevis tourist route," made it sound a lot easier than it was. The hike was ten miles long, with scenery and landscape that stole Everleigh's breath away. Everleigh remembered what her grandmother's journal said about the place: "I haven't experienced complete silence before. The clouds swirled by, the sun was warm, and no one else was there. I think it was as close to heaven on earth as I've experienced."

Hours on, Everleigh made it to the top of Ben Nevis, feeling perhaps the greatest sense of accomplishment in her young life to date. She took more pictures of the vast landscape and paused for a moment to take in the majestic views from the top and snap pictures of herself with the beautiful range behind her. She had done it; she had hiked Ben Nevis! After spending time meditating and enjoying the quiet of being alone, Everleigh noticed the other hikers seemed to be far behind her. She was still alone on the mountaintop, and it had seemed like it had been so for hours. After taking all of the photos she wanted, breathing fresh air, and watching the clouds swirl by in complete silence, Everleigh thought it was time to head back. She started her descent, which was slow because of all the uneven surfaces.

When she finally reached the hostel, she was exhausted and her knees hurt from the distance and the pounding of the rocks on the way down. She had to pat herself on the back for a job well done and for pushing herself to limits she had not physically pushed herself to before. After a full day of hiking, Everleigh enjoyed visiting with fellow hikers who had descended this magnificent mountain like she had that day. It was great to connect with others who were also seeing all of this for the first time. It had been an excellent choice to stop here on her way to the Isle of Skye. She knew she would have to leave early in the morning the next day to make the ferry. She prepacked her stuff, set her alarm, and slept soundly. The alarm went off with a great sound and Everleigh jumped out of her slumber, panicked to think she was late. Still in a dream state, she wondered where she was since she was so exhausted from climbing Ben Nevis. Then everything started coming back to her, and she realized she needed to get dressed and cycle to the ferry.

Everleigh barely made it in time to catch the ferry to the Isle Of Skye. She left her bike at the dock since the rental had expired. On the other side she saw a place to rent bikes; the attendant warned her that taking a bus might be better because the Cuillin Mountains pass was quite challenging and very "hilly." "This mountain range is not for beginners," he said, but Everleigh had known it would be challenging and got on the bike and rode away. She found the more she pushed herself in these challenges, the more she grew, and she was determined not to walk her bike. She would push herself until she found a good spot to have lunch.

After a few hours of grueling uphill pedaling, Everleigh rounded a corner and saw a large red phone box! In the middle of nowhere there was a phone! She wondered if it worked, and she pulled out her international phone card to make a call. Not realizing in Washington the time was eight hours earlier, she called Bradley; he was just getting out of bed, he answered the phone quickly and happy. The excitement in his voice came through the phone. He was so happy to hear from her, and she was relieved when he said so. She asked how he was and how things were at home. She had been thinking how nice it would be to see Bradley and to ask him if he would be interested in meeting her somewhere in Europe. They both said at the same time, "What about Paris?" They laughed and made plans to meet there in about six weeks at the Shangri-La Hotel, which was just down the street from the Arc de Triomphe and had stunning views of the Eiffel Tower. Bradley did have some much-needed vacation time, and he had always wanted to see Paris, so he said he would make the arrangements. After hanging up, Everleigh realized how lonely she was. She delighted in knowing she would see a friendly face soon, but she was also excited because it was her brother, and she needed to see family. She hadn't thought about Bradley much since being in Europe, and it was a lot to process to suddenly have a new person in her life who was her brother.

Everleigh finally made it over the Cuillin Mountains and onto the Isle of Skye. She arrived in Portree, the capital, which was a beautiful little village with jagged cliffs and multi-colored homes that reflected the calm sea water. The village was quaint and charming, and it was a good place to let her body rest after the hike and cycling over a mountain range. The photo opportunities in the little village were spectacular, so Everleigh wandered and took photos in the evening after finding a very quaint hostel. The people were very nice and interested in her journey. She was exhausted by the time she hit her pillow and slept very soundly.

After a few days of rest, it was off to Edinburgh, her last place in Scotland before taking the ferry crossing to Amsterdam, where she would finally be in mainland Europe.

CHAPTER 12

Everleigh couldn't believe she was traveling to Amsterdam! She knew it meant another trip by water, but the chance of her having two horrible sea trips seemed low. She purchased her ticket and got settled on board. The water was choppy as the boat pulled out and headed toward Rotterdam. Everleigh sipped her water and hoped it wouldn't be this way for the entire five-plus hours. She really wanted to rest.

Her hopes were dashed. The sea was rough, and the boat was rocking and swaying with every swell. There was no way she could sleep through a lurch or crash of water against the boat. After hours of battling the sea, the ferry arrived in Rotterdam, and Everleigh, grateful to be on land again, looked for a bus to Amsterdam and the hostel where she planned to stay. She found the bus stop but made a detour into the restroom to throw up first.

Unfortunately, Everleigh had never gotten her sea legs. Luckily, the roads were much smoother than the water, so she arrived in Amsterdam unscathed. After checking in at the hostel, she stopped in a "coffee shop" and quickly realized it was a marijuana bar; there were so many of them, and all claiming to be the crème de la crème of cannabis. Everleigh had never smoked marijuana or even thought about trying it, so she quickly moved on to find a cup of coffee and some breakfast. Even though these "coffee shops" had "special cakes," she opted for some *el fresco* dining on a croissant and tea (she wasn't ready for anything beyond that), and then she made her way to the Van Gogh Museum. The area was hard to navigate, so she got lost more than once trying to find the place. Everleigh was always impressed by Van Gogh's work and decided to visit the museum that houses the largest collection of Van Gogh's paintings and drawings in the world. She was amazed at the artist's brilliance and a bit sad that his life had been so lonely and unsettling. She had a docent take her picture at the entrance so she could put it in a photo album later on since this beautiful museum had not been here when her grandmother was, but from what Everleigh knew about her grandmother, she had enjoyed art. Deciding not to waste time getting lost, Everleigh opted for a tour on a small boat that would take her through the canals of Amsterdam. *At least it isn't atsea,* she thought.

Everleigh laughed when she still ended up with a rough ride. The driver must have stopped into one of those "coffee shops" before getting to work because he was steering erratically. He drove into a piling, causing glasses to fall, people to spill off their seats, and tables to move from one side of the boat to the other. The driver didn't say a word; he just kept driving, while the passengers collected their belongings from the floor and repositioned their tables and chairs and got situated in their original positions. There were broken glasses and upset old ladies, but he never looked back. Everleigh managed to stay upright, but she had to chase down some of her belongings. After two rough ferry rides, she thought a little tour of the canals would be more pleasant, but here she was hanging on for dear life.

Once the tour ended, Everleigh got onto dry land as fast as she could and immediately swore off all future boat or ferry travel, unless absolutely necessary.

As soon as Everleigh returned to the hostel, she decided to check out the sites in Amsterdam and go to the Vondelpark, which was the street right outside of her hostel; it was so convenient she could just walk to the bands. The area had live concerts at this time of year, and different genres of music were being performed on every block! She was offered marijuana several times by passersby as she walked to the different bands, but she declined. There were people everywhere enjoying music and each other's company. Despite being a bit lonely and having a few setbacks on the trip, this was the first time she had thought longer than a few moments of Seattle and home. But she rested in the fact that soon she would see Bradley and have a connection with home and a small piece of her family that was left.

With a new day, Everleigh's elation over Amsterdam began to fade, and she put her thoughts on her next quest. She would travel by train using the Rail Pass she purchased at Central Station in the heart of the city.

Once inside the train station, Everleigh looked at the reader board that was clicking away above the attendant's head and saw a sign that read *Brussels*. She had intended to go there, and now was as good a time as any. She purchased her ticket and waited on the platform for the train to roll in. In a few minutes, she was on her way to Belgium.

Several hours later, Everleigh said a quick prayer of thanks for a smooth trip and got off the train. She immediately found a restroom to use and took the opportunity to splash some water on her face. She came out and headed away from the train station toward town.

However, it seemed she had gone the wrong way. Nothing she had expected to see appeared. She quickly turned around and headed in the other direction. At home, she could always reference the Puget Sound to know which direction was west. But here she had no directional reference. As she was passing by the train station again, she saw her problem. In her rush to get off the train, she was at the south train station, not the north.

Things didn't look too good. This was obviously not a safe part of Brussels. Everleigh looked around for someone to ask for directions. She approached a woman waiting for the next train.

"Excuse me," Everleigh said. "Can you tell me the fastest way to get to the north station?" Instead of any sort of answer, the woman seemed extremely angry and nearly spat at her, speaking what Everleigh thought was Flemish.

The only thing Everleigh understood was that the woman didn't seem too fond of Americans. Everleigh figured out north from the train station map and started to walk in that direction. She continued to get a bit turned around, and along the way, she received more than her share of catcalls. One man asked her to marry him, and another asked her something that, based on his hand gestures, she was glad she didn't understand. She wandered around for about an hour and started to wonder if she'd ever get to the hostel. Hot and tired, she stopped for a drink from a water fountain.

Navigating a foreign country on her own was always going to have a bit of a steep learning curve, but Everleigh was getting better at it every day. After all, she had discovered her mistake quickly and figured out where she needed to go. She took another deep breath and made her way down the stairs.

It was starting to get dark, and she knew she couldn't stay where she was, but she felt she was close to the hostel. She made it to the bottom of the stairs, adjusted her backpack, and moved her second bag to her other hand. She looked both ways, didn't see anyone, and hot-footed it farther north. It wasn't long before she saw some of the places she had read were near the hostel. She saw a street sign that was like a beacon, informing her she was indeed on the right road. She eventually found and rushed through the door of the hostel.

Luckily for her, it seemed no one was paying attention to the crazed and frazzled-looking American girl. As Everleigh was checking in, she noticed the hostel had its own bar in the lobby area. That was just what she needed right now, a drink! She dumped her bags in her new room and quickly returned for a glass of wine. She found a small table off to the side where only someone really looking for her could find her. She practically breathed in the wine and could feel herself start to relax. She promptly ordered a bottle and figured she could take anything left up to her room. By the time the bottle was about two-thirds empty, Everleigh felt better, buzzed but better. She was questioning her travel skills, but she was proud of herself for making it to the hostel, despite the wrong train station and grumpy people.

CHAPTER 13

Everleigh next took a train to Bruges, Belgium, because she'd seen so many photos of it. Her grandmother had been there, and she was ready to see the beautiful pictures in real life. She booked a round-trip ticket and was on her way. As she settled into her seat, she pulled out her grandmother's journal and reread her entry:"Bruges is the most beautiful place I have seen so far. The cobblestone streets and the ornately decorated houses along the canals…it's like a fairy tale!"

A fairy tale that sounded perfect to Everleigh. The train ride was blessedly uneventful, and she double-checked the train station before she got off. When she saw a bike rental location, she decided to rent a bike and tour the city in a way she would really enjoy that was also a great way to see the sights. She headed out on her two-wheeled tour and made sure to find the Church of Our Lady, where her grandmother had taken a few photos. Michelangelo's sculpture of Madonna and Child took her breath away. The quaint cobblestone streets, the amazing Gothic architecture, and the charm all made Everleigh agree it was the most beautiful place she'd seen so far—plus she enjoyed the scrumptious chocolate that Belgium was known for. By the end of the day, she was starving and thrilled to find a warm and friendly restaurant where she enjoyed a bowl of Bolognese pasta. It was such a respite that she opted to stay overnight and head back to Brussels in the morning. The next day, after a strong cup of coffee and a big breakfast, she boarded the train to return to Brussels.

Everleigh knew once she got back to Brussels, she would travel on to Germany. On the train back to Brussels, she stared out the window to take in the view and daydream. No real thoughts were coming into focus; she just kept jumping from one emotion to another, one issue to another. She was unsure how she felt about Bradley joining her in Paris. She pushed the thoughts out of her mind as the ticket agent made his way down the aisle. Everleigh pulled out her bag and searched for her ticket. Round trip, no problem.

"Ticket, please," the agent said as he walked slowly down the aisle, stopping at each occupied seat. When he arrived at Everleigh's seat, she handed her ticket to him. He took a quick look and handed it back.

"No good," he said.

"Yes, it's good," Everleigh replied. "It's a round-trip ticket."

"American?"

"Yes, is that a problem?" she asked, annoyed by his tone.

"No problem. I will speak English for you. Your ticket is not good for today."

"What? It's a round-trip ticket!"

"Round trip for yesterday, not today. You need to buy a ticket for today's train."

"That's ridiculous. I'm not going to pay for that. I've already paid for a round-trip ticket. What's the difference if it's yesterday or today?"

"You need to buy a ticket or get off the train."

"No..." was all Everleigh said. She felt she was being taken advantage of as an American. The ticket agent took out a badge and flashed it at her. Then he asked for her passport.

"No," she repeated.

"Then you'll have to get off the train."

They continued to argue, and the other passengers began looking at her. Everleigh was being threatened by the agent that he would remove her from the train. There was no way that was going to happen; she wanted to get back to Brussels and get out of this country. It was a good thing that thought stayed in her head. Bashing the country she was in probably wouldn't win her friends. The ticket agent spoke to someone on his radio, but not in English, so she wasn't sure what he said.

Everleigh was sure she had become one of those crazy Americans; sometimes she could be like a dog with a bone—a little too stubborn— but she realized she was making a scene and had zero desire to be looked at as an "ugly American." She grabbed money out of her pack and shoved it toward the agent. He took it and moved on to check other tickets. Everleigh was angry and embarrassed.

She slumped down in her seat near the window and stared out of it the entire rest of the trip, doing her best to avoid eye contact with anyone. When they pulled into the station, she rushed off the train and back to the hostel.

Time to get out of this country as fast as possible. She collected her things and headed back to the train station. She caught the train to Nuremberg, Germany. It took almost seven hours to get there; Everleigh sat reflecting on her day as the beautiful scenery whisked by her window. By early afternoon, she hopped off the train, found a hostel, and set out to see the town. She had heard so many great things about Germany and especially the beer gardens and the warmth of the people. After being in Brussels, a curmudgeon would be considered nice.

After Bruges, Nuremberg seemed overwhelmingly huge. Everleigh felt small, but resolute. She'd had a few bumpy days, but overall, she was doing well. Despite almost getting kicked off the train to Brussels, she was proud she had stood up for herself at least initially. But better to buy a ticket than get stranded somewhere.

Everleigh made her way to a nearby hostel and hung out in the lobby area while deciding what to do the following day. Bradley kept popping into her head, but she figured any questions they would have for each other would be best addressed in person. She was excited and nervous for his arrival, but uncertain what to expect. All of that would wait until Paris; she would focus on enjoying each place she visited until then, staying in the moment. She was lost in all these thoughts when a woman about her age approached her.

"Is this chair taken?"

Everleigh looked up and saw a young woman with a crown of red hair flowing around her. The light from behind her made it glow. Her friendly smile was topped with sparkling eyes. Her accent and appearance made Everleigh think she must be Irish.

"No, it's not. Please have a seat," Everleigh replied.

"Thank you. I'm exhausted. I've been on the road all day," the woman said, sitting down.

"I just arrived from Belgium myself. I'm so tired I just decided to sit for a while."

"I haven't been there yet," said the woman. "What's it like?"

"I loved Bruges; it's one of the most beautiful places I've ever been. The whole place is just charming and friendly, and lots of great food."

"I have to check it out. I've just been in Switzerland."

"Did you enjoy it?"

"I loved it. The cities are very compact, so it's easy to see everything; there is so much nature everywhere—lakes, mountains, parks. I think Lake Geneva was my favorite area. It's just stunning."

"It sounds wonderful. I'm Everleigh, by the way."

"I'm Eileen. Nice to meet you. May I ask where you're from? I'm guessing America, right?"

"Right. It's not something I can hide. I'm from Washington state, Seattle to be exact. And you?"

"Ireland. A little town outside Dublin."

"I loved Ireland. I visited Dublin, Belfast, and Galway."

"I work in Dublin but take a train from Dalkey. That's my village. So how long are you staying here?"

"I'm not sure yet. I'm trying to figure that out."

"Same here. I've been traveling alone, and I have to tell you it can be a bit overwhelming."

"What do you mean?"

"I love all the freedom, but I guess I'm getting tired of having to make every decision and not having anyone to share my adventures with. Does that make sense?"

"It does. I'm traveling alone, too. Every day is great, but some moments are really hard."

"So, you get it! I haven't wanted to even say it out loud when I call home. My folks told me not to go alone, but I'm stubborn. So, I tell them everything is just sunshine and lollipops, you know? Nothing about getting lost or scared or spending too much money because I just got swindled at some shop."

"Oh, I've had some of that, too." Everleigh laughed. "But here we are, still alive and traveling, right?"

"Right! Can I ask you a favor?"

"Sure."

"You seem so nice. Do you think we could do some sightseeing together tomorrow? I would love to have someone to talk with and find places with."

"And maybe get lost with?"

"Exactly! What do you think?"

"I'd love that," said Everleigh. "Are you okay with an early start?"

"No problem."

"Great. I'll meet you here at six o'clock. Does that work?"

"Perfect. Oh, Everleigh, thank you so much."

"I'm looking forward to having a touring buddy, too."

Everleigh said goodbye to her new friend and then bought a few pieces of fruit and some crackers that were available in the hostel's lobby before she made her way upstairs for a quiet night in anticipation of a bright and early morning. She wanted to read through her grandmother's journal again too.

The entire next day seemed to be focused on amazing historic sites and tasty treats, not that Everleigh ever complained about food or beautiful architecture. Her appetite seemed more voracious than usual, maybe because she had a dining companion, or maybe the food in Germany really was just great; either way, it was a total win.

Eileen and Everleigh started their day at a nearby café with fresh pastries, jellies, and bread, and they washed their food down with copious amounts of steeping hot tea. After devouring their plethora of tasty treats, they wandered through the town square and went on a tour of the Imperial Castle of Nuremberg. It easily could have taken an entire day to see all of it. The castle was one of the more stunning pieces of architecture Everleigh had seen so far, and it had stood there since the Middle Ages, with its high ceilings, long pillars, and beautiful marble. The castle is considered to be one of the most formidable medieval fortifications in Europe.

By the time they got to Erlangen, it was late, and live music was blaring, the wine was flowing, and a food festival was in full swing. The German food booths were amazing, and they both ended up eating more than they thought possible. The two were laughing at everything, enjoying the evening, and taking pictures of each other in front of nearly every building they came upon. It was late, and they both felt ready to head back to the hostel. Everleigh told Eileen a bit about her grandmother's trip as they walked. Eileen was fascinated and wanted to be a part of exploring the sights her grandmother had seen.

"Let's call it a night and head to Bamberg tomorrow," Eileen suggested as they entered the hostel lobby.

"I'm about to pass out standing up," said Everleigh. "I'd better get to bed."

"I'm right behind you," Eileen said as they teetered toward the stairs.

Right before she was out for the night, Everleigh had the thought that she was going to be fine and that having Eileen to pal around with was just what she needed to shake off her loneliness. Tomorrow, Bamberg.

The next morning, Everleigh and Eileen made their way back to the train station. Everleigh loved how easy it was to travel by train in Europe. No worries about driving, getting lost, or parking! They would have to travel farther than yesterday, but it was only a thirty-minute ride on a direct train. They bought their tickets and waited for their train to arrive. Once on board, they settled into seats and talked about the places they would check out.

"My grandmother loved churches and cathedrals, so I do want to check out some of them."

"Absolutely, and let's check out that rose garden. What's it called?"

"Rosengarten!"

"Well, you'd think I could remember that," Eileen said as they both laughed.

The train ride was over before they knew it. Then they had about a fifteen-minute walk into the center of town. The place was filled with history at every corner—not surprising for being more than one-thousand-years old. The first stop they made was Bamberg Cathedral where Eileen took a picture of Everleigh by the same stained-glass window where her grandmother was photographed so many years before.

The cathedral was a bit overdone for Everleigh's taste with all the gold touches and ornate fixtures, although that didn't dampen her excitement to know she was standing in yet another place Grandma Susan had once stood. They moved on to check out a couple of museums and the Rosengarten, part of Neue Residenz, the largest palace in the city. It was a gorgeous garden with statuary and rose bushes of every sort. They stopped and rested on one of the nearby benches. It was late afternoon, and the sun was slipping behind gathering clouds.

"I'm so thirsty!" Everleigh exclaimed. "Do you want some water?"

"Yes, but I was actually thinking about something icy cold. Let's go check out a beer garden."

"That sounds perfect."

They got up and walked toward a nearby bier garten. The clouds that had started to gather turned dark, and before they reached the garden, it started to rain. Just a few drops at first, but it quickly became a steady rainfall. They started to walk faster and ran the last block. Wet, hot, and hungry, they dashed through the gate and found a seat in the bier garten under a canopy, but the wind was blowing and they were getting soaked. The rain finally subsided and they were able to relax in the sun and dry out.

A server came up to take their order. Eileen ordered right away. Everleigh wasn't sure what she wanted, but she picked a Weissbier off the list that she felt she could pronounce. Everleigh had been practicing ordering menu items in German, so she asked the server in German for a small stein of beer.

"What size?" the server replied in English in a sarcastic tone.

"Oh, a small stein, please."

"You come back when you're thirsty," he replied. Everleigh was not sure whether he was serious, but Eileen certainly got a chuckle out of the exchange.

"Okay, okay...a large stein, then!" Everleigh said through laughter.

They ordered food and enjoyed the festive atmosphere. After a few hours, they walked in the warm evening air, which felt really good. Everleigh was truly having a wonderful time. Everleigh really wanted to go to Berlin and experience all of the history there, so she asked Eileen if she would be interested in visiting with her since they seemed to meld together so well. Eileen had not considered Berlin as part of her travels, but she was excited at the opportunity to go to Berlin and with Everleigh, who was so adventurous. They went back to their hostel and decided to take a car service to Berlin the next day.

In the morning, Everleigh and Eileen checked out of their hostel and went to a nearby café for coffee. Everleigh had grabbed a brochure for a private car service to Berlin. It was cheaper than two train tickets, so they opted for that route. The private car driver was a woman who clearly thought she was Mario Andretti. Once she hit the autobahn, she raced her VW toward Berlin at well over 100 miles an hour.

The two held on tight in the backseat and wondered if paying more for the train would have been a better idea; for sure, it would have felt safer. Still, they decided to sit back and enjoy their crazy driver, who smoked up a storm and cussed in perfect English. In record time, she dropped them off in front of a war-torn hostel.

"It looks like a bomb went off here," Everleigh said as she and Eileen got out of the car.

"It did," the driver said. "This place was bombed during the war, and they're just now starting to fix it up." She sorted out their payment, waved, and lit up another cigarette as she raced off down the road. They checked into the hostel and learned that the renovations had been held back in part because of Berlin and East Germany's separation from Western Europe during the Cold War. There was scaffolding and construction cloth and cranes everywhere along the street. Everleigh was glad to see they were fixing things up, but because the hostel was in the middle of the project, there were no bathrooms on their floor. No worries; with the two of them together, Everleigh and Eileen didn't mind traipsing up to another floor to use the bathroom there.

In the morning, they decided to take a walking tour of Berlin. It didn't start until two o'clock in the afternoon, so they had plenty of time for a good meal and a load of laundry before hitting the road. At the starting point of the tour, their tour guide, Tony, made sure everyone knew what to expect before taking their money.

"This could be a twelve-hour tour," Tony said, laughing. "Seriously, it is about five hours of walking, so I hope you all have on comfortable shoes."

"Good thing I brought my comfy shoes," Eileen said.

"Good thing I washed my comfortable pants!" Everleigh replied.

Berlin had so much rich history, and it really was a beautiful and bustling city. The mood turned darker when Tony took them to the area where Hitler's bunker had been and where he had committed suicide. The actual bunker was not preserved, but the spot was noted so people would always remember. Then they went to the site of the Sunken Library in Bebelplatz, where the Nazis' German Student Union burned 20,000 books in May of 1933. Many of the authors were persecuted writers who had left Germany and gone into exile. What a stunning piece of German history.

Then Tony took them to an amazing Italian restaurant. Surprised to find good Italian food, Everleigh and Eileen and their group ordered different dishes to share with each other from their walking tour group. They were making fast friends with this group, and because most were fellow backpackers, they got along great and had a lot in common. By this time, they had been on the walking tour for about five hours, but everyone wanted to keep it going. There was so much to learn about Germany, including the beer.

"Now to a wonderful pub and what this country is known for—beer!" said Tony as he led the group to a very local-looking place down a back alley—a place most tourists would never find. It was clear he brought most of his groups here because everyone inside seemed to know him.

"Play darts with me," Everleigh asked Eileen as they sipped on huge steins of beer. "I've never played."

"Me either, so we're even."

"I just hope I don't hit anyone," said Everleigh.

A few patrons joined them, and despite not speaking good English, they were able to converse with them and even bought them a round of beer. By the time they had all had their fill and the group headed out the door, Tony realized they had missed the last train, so they would have to walk all the way back to the hostel. They took a more direct route than earlier in the day, but it was still a long walk. By the time

Everleigh and Eileen walked into the front door, it was two in the morning. It really had been a twelve-hour tour!

The next day, Everleigh and Eileen explored Berlin on their own. The East Side Gallery, considered the longest open-air gallery in the world, was fascinating. The gallery runs along the Spree River and contains the longest section of the Berlin Wall in existence. They took a lot of pictures at Checkpoint Charlie where people had crossed over from East Germany to the American Sector.

Finally, they made their way to a German restaurant where they ordered schnitzel and beer. It was their last night in Berlin so they wanted the local flare.

"It's been so great having someone to tour around with," Eileen told Everleigh. "Thanks again for agreeing to let me tag along with you."

"Thank you. I think I did more with you than I might have on my own."

"Want to do more?"

"What do you mean?"

"Come with me to Vienna!"

"What?" asked Everleigh, surprised by the invitation.

"Come with me to Vienna."

"That's not on my itinerary. I was going to move on to Poland."

"You can do that after Vienna. Come on; we're having such a great time, and I would love to have your company for a few more days."

"Well…"

"Come on. You don't have a tight schedule. You just have a list of places you want to visit to relive your grandmother's trip. Make Vienna a stop just for you."

"I do like that idea, and we are having a blast together."

"So, you'll come!"

"That wasn't a question, was it?"

"Nope!"

"Okay,   let's   do   it!"

CHAPTER 14

"Hi Everleigh, I'm confirmed for Paris."

A very succinct email from Bradley awaited Everleigh when she finally managed to stop at an internet cafe to check her email. She hadn't done it enough during her trip, and messages were piling up in her inbox; however, she knew she would have plenty of time to return every message when she returned home. The only pertinent message was this one, so she and Bradley could email back and forth to arrange their meeting in Paris.

After checking both the bus and train schedule, Everleigh convinced Eileen to travel by bus to Vienna. It was only about thirty minutes longer and one-fourth the price. Either way, the bulk of the day would be spent traveling, and they knew the bus made enough stops for them to stretch their legs. So, they bought tickets, shoved their bags in the overhead rack, and settled in for the ride. Eileen quickly fell asleep, but Everleigh spent most of the time staring out the window to soak in all the sights. She was more than a bit excited to veer off her planned itinerary and have no journal entries or notes to guide her.

As the bus traveled south, one of the stops was in Dresden, Germany, where they were able to get off the bus and walk around for an hour. The bus station was in the heart of this architecturally stunning city. Everleigh and Eileen walked around taking as many photos of Dresden as they could. The city had been bombed during World War II, which had destroyed the entire city center. As they came around a corner, they saw a church steeple that had been half blown off. The city seemed to intend to keep it that way in memory of the war. It made for an amazing photo. This picturesque city had so much history and was well worth the stop. Just an hour and a half south was

Prague, a city Everleigh had dreamed of seeing since she was a young girl. She'd heard stories of it looking like something out of a children's fairy tale.

Prague was as picturesque as Everleigh had imagined, but even better in person; she was so keyed up to be in Prague for the first time, but she also felt immediate peace and comfort in the city. She felt almost like she was at home; it was an odd feeling, but a nice one, nonetheless. Everleigh had always *had* a home, but she had never felt at home.

Everleigh finally understood the difference in this moment; she was very comfortable. She and Eileen wandered into a local pub to try absinthe in Prague rather than anywhere else in Europe, and they were both eager to experience it with each other.

They sat at the bar and watched as their bartender poured the toxic-waste-colored green liquor over a spoon with a sugar cube placed ever so delicately above a candle. This was done to dilute the drink a little; apparently, it would be too strong to drink straight. Although Everleigh had heard of absinthe sometimes being a psychoactive "drug," neither she nor Eileen had an unpleasant experience or any hallucinations. They did, however, get good and properly drunk on what they now learned to be nicknamed "The Green Faerie." Eileen grabbed them some food while Everleigh made her way to the restroom. By the time she got out, Eileen was urging her to hurry because they had lost track of time and she realized their bus was about to leave. Everleigh threw her bag over her shoulder and started to run toward the bus, behind Eileen. Her sandal got hung up in the uneven cobblestone pavers, and before she knew it, she was flying face-first toward the ground.

Everleigh fell so fast that her skirt flew up, and by the time she landed, she was flashing her thong underwear and most of her butt to everyone at the station. She hustled herself back on her feet and felt the burn of embarrassment over her entire body. She wanted to run and hide, but before she could move, Eileen appeared in a flash, grabbed her hand, and ran with her to get on the bus. She didn't let go until they'd settled in their seats. There were a few small smiles and side glances from a handful of passengers, but it seemed most of the passengers hadn't seen her fall or didn't care. They flopped into their seats and Everleigh hid her face in her hands. Then she heard Eileen giggling.

"I had no idea you were such an exhibitionist," Eileen said, trying to stifle her laughter.

"Neither did I," Everleigh replied, covering her face with her hands.

"Don't be embarrassed," said Eileen. "At least you were wearing a clean thong."

Still mortified, Everleigh glanced over to see Eileen's face was barely suppressing a grin. Her grin grew and she let out a huge burst of joyous laughter. Everleigh wasn't feeling it at first, but Eileen elbowed her and kept laughing. Finally, Everleigh found the humor in the entire incident, helped along by the bus now making its way down the road and away from the site of her spill. She joined in the giggles until she had laughed so hard that her face began to ache. They did not stop laughing for a long time. It was the incident, the absinthe, and the pure joy of being with a newfound friend.

As they arrived in Vienna, Everleigh was agog at the city's beauty. Every building seemed historical, and every street was quaint and charming. They decided to put the money they'd saved on bus tickets toward a real hotel. The idea of a real hotel room and a private bath made them practically giddy. After getting settled into their room, they looked out the window to see a crowd gathering for a parade. Unbeknownst to them, they had arrived on the night of a huge gay pride parade. Everleigh had seen smaller versions back in Seattle, but the bright colors, lavish costumes, and pageantry of this one made it one of the most spectacular, over-the-top, celebratory parades she'd ever seen. They loved it and were sorry to see it end, but their empty stomachs were happy when they found a place to enjoy a nice meal.

"There are so many museums and gardens. I'm not sure where to start," Eileen said as she thumbed through a tourist brochure while they waited for their food.

"Here's a walking tour."

"After our Berlin walking tour experience, I'm thinking we should get tickets for the Hop-On Hop-Off bus. We can see what we want, rest when we need, and really get a lay of the city."

"That sounds perfect. I don't think I could handle another twelve-hour walk anyway."

They found a stand where they bought tickets and only had to wait a few minutes before a bus stopped to pick them up. It was a beautiful day, so they opted to sit on the top deck of the bus with the open-air windows. It wasn't too crowded, so they each sat by a window and stuck their heads out, looking exactly like the tourists they were. Everleigh snapped photos of every building along the way. They jumped off near St. Stephen's Cathedral. Even though her grandmother hadn't come to Vienna, Everleigh felt pulled to take in one of the city's churches.

They visited the Belvedere Museum and the Natural History Museum. They ended their tour with a stop at an open-air market and sipped on the best Viennese coffee they had ever tasted! That night, the pride celebration continued through Stadtpark in the heart of the city. Nearby and just off the park, they found an unbelievable dueling piano concert at Intermezzo Bar, and a live play, *Carmina Burana*, along with several other acts and entertainment along their journey. After being thoroughly entertained, they realized they were starving!

Nearby was a busy restaurant brimming with happy people eating plates brimming with wonderful sausage dinners. Everleigh and Eileen were seated and took the server's recommendations for food and beer.

Then, though stuffed to the gills, they were coerced by their server to indulge in some of the popular chocolate desserts. A good choice for sure. They walked back to their hotel full of great food and wonderful memories.

"I have had so much fun with you, Everleigh," Eileen said as they each sprawled out on their respective beds.

"Me, too. I am so glad I met you, and I'm even happier I came to Vienna with you. What a gorgeous place."

"Let's promise to stay in touch, okay?"

"Absolutely!"

"I have to head back to Ireland tomorrow. I have to get back to work soon and want to be sure I'm home in time to get settled, you know?"

"I do. I quit my job just before I left for Europe, and it's been odd not working. Since my mom died, so much has changed."

"I can't imagine how that feels. I'm pretty close to my mum."

"I was, too," said Everleigh. "I lived with her."

"Right, I remember you told me. So, do you miss it? Home?"

"Hmm...sometimes but mostly, no."

"And work?"

"Not so much." Everleigh laughed. Eileen joined her.

"I love all the people at work," said Eileen, "but I don't always love the actual work."

"Isn't that the truth?" said Everleigh. "What time do you have to leave tomorrow?"

"I'm going to take the early bus back into Germany. Then, I'll probably grab a train and finally a ferry back to Dublin. It's faster and cheaper to fly, but I *hate* flying. Besides, it gives me a bit of time to see a few more sites along the way."

"I like your way instead of flying. I'd rather stay on the ground. What time is the bus?"

"Eight. There's one at about 4:45, but that's just too early!"

"Eight is early enough. Do you want to have an early breakfast before you go?"

"There's no need for you to get up early. Just sleep in a bit," said Eileen.

"I think I will. I think I'll take the day to plan out the rest of my trip and not worry about leaving until the day after tomorrow."

"That sounds brilliant."

The two continued to chat as Eileen packed up for her early morning exit. They ordered some tea and cookies from room service to celebrate their friendship without risking a traveling hangover for Eileen. When they turned out the light, Everleigh found herself looking forward to planning out the rest of her trip. She wanted to reconnect with her grandmother's journals and plan places to visit and stay. She wondered about Italy, Spain, and Paris, but knew she'd do fine navigating without any kind of guide. Thinking of Paris made her think of Bradley.

Everleigh hadn't thought of him for the past few days; he was one piece of her life she hadn't shared with Eileen.

The next morning, when Everleigh awoke, Eileen was already gone. The room was quiet. Everleigh was alone again. This time she didn't feel lonely. Instead, she felt strong and self-assured. She got up and readied herself for the day. She checked at the front desk to be sure she was checked in for another night. After that, she found a nearby café with outdoor seating, different from the one she and Eileen had visited. She settled into a comfy chair, ordered breakfast, and began reading in the journal she had tucked into her bag:

> *I wasn't sure I wanted to go to Poland, but at the last minute I decided it is just what I need to do. There is so much tragic history there with everything that happened to the Jewish people during World War II. I pray we never have another war like that, another person like Hitler. Well, anyway, I think I need to go see both the dark and light of this country. The darkness of the past at Auschwitz and Birkenau. The resilience of the Polish people in Krakow. I expect I will never be the same, emerging fully from my protected bubble of life. Still, I relish the experience and the journey.*

Everleigh decided to travel by train to Poland and do the same thing—make herself see Auschwitz and Birkenau. She hated violence and had barely made it through the movie *Schindler's List*, but to deny history is to remain ignorant and likely repeat it. So, she would go. After Poland, she would set her sights on France and Italy for more joyous sites. Everleigh had enjoyed some of the best days of her trip in Germany and Vienna with her new friend, Eileen. Maybe it was just having someone else with you, someone who admitted that traveling alone was a big deal. It was a big deal. She was doing it, not always well, not always gracefully, but she was doing it.

When Everleigh boarded the train to Poland, she was pleasantly surprised to be shown a semi-private cabin. There were seats for others, but so far no one else was in the room. It felt like luxurious travel. She was going to enjoy the next seven to eight hours. It was around two in the afternoon and the train would arrive in Krakow about 9:15 p.m.

Perfect. She had already arranged for her hostel so finding where she would spend the night should be easy.

Everleigh bought some tea and a light snack from the club car and took it back to her cabin. She closed the door and realized there were no curtains to close, only a little door latch for privacy. She settled in to enjoy the ride and soon nodded off.

Everleigh woke to the feeling that someone was watching her, and in fact, there was. Her eyes traveled up to his. A man was standing outside her door, staring at her. He was not subtle nor discrete, in the slightest; it immediately gave Everleigh chills. She could see the door was still closed and latched, so she opted to ignore him. She grabbed something to read and looked away. She really wished there was a curtain to shut him out because her not-so-subtle hint by digging into her book did not seem to deter him. When she glanced up, he was still there.

Ignoring him didn't seem to make him go away, so she just stared back at him. She gave him her best "Don't mess with me" look. She was not sure if it would work, but after a few moments, he walked away.

Everleigh breathed a sigh of relief and put the book she had been holding down beside her. She took a few deep breaths and relaxed. She got up to check outside the door and looked both ways down the train corridor. He was gone and probably wasn't coming back. She picked up the book and started to read. Before she knew it, the sun was down, it was dark outside, and her cabin was dim. The overhead light she had on for reading turned off on its own. Before she could even turn her head toward the cabin door, she knew she wasn't alone.

She felt him before she saw him. The creepy guy was back, and he wasn't just a watcher. His hands were all over her. He had broken through the flimsy latch and was waiting for her to be unsuspecting. She could feel his beefy hands attempting to paw at her under her shirt and reach up under her bra. She struggled against him, but while she was no wimp, the man was strong, much stronger than she was.

He grabbed at her pants and pulled at the button and zipper. They were open and Everleigh felt more vulnerable and afraid than she ever had. His hot breath was on her neck, and she looked fervently toward the open door, hoping someone would walk by. Hoping someone would help.

There was no one there.

He started to put his hand down her underwear and Everleigh began to scream. He clamped his hand over her mouth. She smelled his sweat; he was so close to her, and he was so large that even the slightest attempt to move away from him seemed impossible. Everleigh's mind went blank. She figured if no one could see her, they would have to hear her. She was overcome with anger and despair. She almost felt dumbfounded that somebody could feel entitled to treat her this way. She saw flashes of images—what she imagined her mother's rape had been like. Maybe it hadn't been much different than this. Maybe she had tried to fight and wasn't strong enough. Words from her grandma's letter flashed in her mind: "When your mother was just a teenager, she was very sweet and naïve...but it wasn't the dreamy evening she deserved. It was a nightmare instead."

A white-hot anger overtook Everleigh; she bit the man's fingers and screamed as loudly as she could. She, herself, had nothing to be embarrassed about. *He* was the one attacking *her*. It was not a frightened scream either, but an angry scream. One full of years of feeling less than, from moment to moment, day by day—one of smaller anger and incidences that come from having to live as a woman in a blatantly sexist world. It was the buildup of twenty-six years of this anger and neglect, and the cherry on top was knowing how she had been brought into this world by violence, through force. Her mother had never deserved that. Hell, Everleigh herself didn't deserve it. Neither did Bradley. One man's actions had been responsible for destroying an entire family.

Months of loss came out too, in the most unusual, guttural yell that had ever come out of Everleigh. The fresh loss of her mother, the loss of her grandmother, and the anger of finding out her life was nothing like what she had thought. A primal scream from a person who had reached her limit. With the anger came a strength like that of those mothers who can pick cars up off their children. She pushed the man off her, and he hit the floor, falling through the cabin door. He was clearly taken aback by her outburst of strength and her screams; he did not want all the attention she was bringing to him.

Everleigh stood up from her seat as he was trying to stand up. She waited to see what he would try next. He didn't leave. Instead, he attempted to lunge at her.

Not knowing she even knew how to fight, she gave him a punch in the gut, followed by a swift and serious kick to the groin. He fell to his knees. She wasn't done. She picked up her bag and brought it down hard on his head. She shouted at him.

"Enough! No more! I will *not* be your victim!"

He didn't move. Everleigh wasn't sure he had even heard what she said, but she didn't care. This was about her. She quickly scooped up her belongings and stepped toward the door, adjusting her hair and clothing back to their proper places. She looked back at the heap of a man on the floor, groaning in pain, and as she walked out, she was relieved to see they were pulling into Krakow. The commotion had caused a few cabin lights to come on and others to spill out into the aisle. Everleigh walked out of her cabin with her head held as high as she could and was relieved to see the porter standing by to help her off the train.

"Thank you, sir. By the way, there's a sick pervert over by my cabin. I'm sure you noticed; you should get him off the train," Everleigh said with more inner strength than she had ever experienced.

"Did he hurt you?" the porter asked with great concern.

"He   tried,   but   I   handled   it."

CHAPTER 15

Everleigh spent the next day walking around Krakow and reading her grandma's journal with a new insight. She had a small, vague map of the area from the front desk at the hostel. It didn't help much except to mark the general area and the hostel location was marked with an X. *At least it will help me find my way back*, she thought, and she shoved it into her coat pocket. She visited Wawel Castle and Wawel Cathedral. She again found the spots where her grandmother had stood and been photographed. She wandered through the Main Market Square and St. Mary's Church, admiring how beautiful everything was.

She then looked for a place to eat. Every place looked so good that it was hard for her to decide where to go, but she found a wonderful restaurant that served pierogies; one look at a plateful being carried to a diner was enough to sell her. She had to try them, and she was glad when she did.

The next day, Everleigh decided to take a bus and venture out to Auschwitz and Birkenau. She knew from history, and her grandmother's journal, that Birkenau was where the Jews had come in on the trains, and that the platform there was where they had been loaded to be sent off to concentration camps. The Auschwitz Museum displayed the uniforms of the workers who dug the ditches and worked in the fields. She photographed a monument that was dedicated to those who had died there. She saw cells where people had been suffocated by being shut in airtight rooms.

Perhaps most jarring was the "death wall" where people were lined up and executed daily, especially those who tried to escape or were sentenced for conspiracy. Everleigh read that some of these people were often sentenced and killed on the same day. It was unnerving to be in a place where the Jewish people and others were worked, starved, and tortured. She was overwhelmed with the atrocities of the Holocaust and wept for people without power and for those who had all lost too much. She sat at the small calm water pond in the center of Auschwitz and tried to feel the atrocities that had happened there. It was a very surreal and heavy experience and very eerily quiet; no one was around her, and there was complete silence. She took a few photos and soaked in the experience of being in such a historically rich place. And she prayed for those who had lost their lives there.

The next day, Everleigh was ready for less emotional sightseeing and walked around the area near the hostel. She meandered and took a lot of photos. She found herself in Main Street Square looking for the tram so she could get out a bit farther. She climbed aboard at dusk.

It didn't take long before she saw they were going through some rough areas with graffiti-covered walls. Clearly, she had gotten on a tram going in the wrong direction. No worries; she would just ride the tram all the way around and get back off at the square. The map was sadly vague with very few street names. Everleigh wasn't sure what to do when the tram stopped and clearly was done for the night. There was no magic loop to get her back to where she had started. Tired and frustrated, and unsure what to do, Everleigh realized it was nearly one in the morning. She was about to cry when she saw the driver, who had turned everything off and locked the doors. She started to wave her red raincoat in front of the tram's window. He didn't even turn around and went into the station office, not seeing her.

Did he just leave me here?

Unsure of what to do, Everleigh waited. Less than ten minutes later, he came back outside and saw her. He panicked and opened the door. She tried to explain her situation to him. He did not speak English, and they both stared at each other and looked back and forth at the map. He gestured that he could help her and brought her into the same tram with him. What else could she do? She needed help in a foreign country, and neither of them spoke the other's language. After her experience on the train getting there, a small part of her was a little unsure what to do. If he were a serial killer, he wasn't being very stealthy, and it seemed as if he wanted to help her, so she trusted him.

As the tram made its way down the track, the driver flagged down a tram going in the opposite direction. Both drivers got out of their trams and began talking. Everleigh got out too, even though she couldn't offer much to the conversation. The first driver asked for her map and showed it to the second driver. After a few minutes of discussion and shaking and nodding of heads, the second driver told her to get on his tram. He managed a few words of English to let her know he was going to take her in the other direction. That was a start and better than standing in the dark. Everleigh hopped on his tram and sat in the seat right behind him.

The tram kept going and going. It was so dark outside, and she could not tell where they were, not that she had any sense of knowing where she was in this country. After about an hour, he stopped and said this was where she needed to get off the tram. It didn't look right at all. None of what she could see seemed familiar. He could tell she was confused, so he got off the tram and pointed down the street toward some lit buildings.

"You're sure the hostel is that way?" she asked.

The driver nodded and smiled and continued to point down the road.

"Thank you," Everleigh said. "Thank you very much." She handed him a few dollars and headed in the direction he pointed.

Just moments later, Everleigh breathed a sigh of relief when she recognized the hostel.

Luckily, the doors were not locked. She entered as quietly as possible. Completely worn out, she made her way to her room and practically passed out in her bed. Everything had worked out; she was safe and back in her bed. She was grateful that the two tram drivers had gone so far out of their way to help her get here. People were good.

Everleigh got up mid-morning and showered. She decided only day trips were an option for today. She wanted to be back to the hostel before dark, just in case. Just outside of Krakow was the Wieliczka Salt Mine where there were a series of underground chambers filled with salt art and carvings created by miners during the 1900s. The immense detail was mind-blowing, especially the chandeliers made of rock salt. She had no idea there could be things of such beauty tucked away underground.

Three days in Poland seemed like enough for Everleigh. She decided she would take the next train to Paris. When she checked the schedule, she realized there was a night train she could still make. Since it was a long trip, she opted not to wait and spend another day in Poland. She packed her bag and got to the station in time to buy her ticket and get on the train. She felt hopeful and joyful as she settled in and headed to Paris. Who wouldn't feel hopeful heading to the city of love?

After a long night in a comfortable sleeping car, Everleigh arrived in one of the many Paris train stations. She took a short walk and found the hotel she and Bradley were set to meet at; it seemed safe enough, and being close to the train station was a bonus. She checked in and settled into her room, waiting for Bradley to call upon his arrival. He had emailed that he would phone her room when he arrived. A few hours passed, and then the phone next to her bed rang:

"Hello?" she said.

"Everleigh, it's Bradley. I'm here and all checked in. This place is gorgeous."

"It is," Everleigh replied. "It's more gorgeous than I imagined."

They both laughed. A laughter that cut through Everleigh's nerves and put her at ease.

Every time Everleigh had a doubt or a thought about this relationship going poorly, she was almost immediately proven wrong. They were similar people and their relationship had been easy since the very first day. She was suddenly filled with happiness rather than trepidation at the thought of her brother being here in Paris. She almost broke into a run to go meet him in the lobby.

"I'm so glad to see you," Bradley said after they spotted each other and hugged.

"I'm glad to see you, too."

"And I'm excited to see things here!" He motioned around them.

"Me too," said Everleigh. "I've been waiting for you so we could sightsee together!"

"I feel honored." He smiled. His lips curled into Grandpa Rogers' smirk. Everleigh couldn't resist hugging him. She threw her arms around his neck, and he warmly returned the hug. It was...easy; it felt right. They withdrew and stared at each other a moment, smiling and slightly nodding to each other. It was the kind of moment that did not need words. They were content to be with each other. Bradley and Everleigh both felt a natural pull to sit down, eat, and talk about their family in more detail. Everleigh knew there would be questions, and she wanted to answer as many of them as possible.

"I'm sure you have questions…." Everleigh figured she would just dive right in.

"Paris is wonderful," Bradley replied, "but yes, I didn't come just for the macarons."

Everleigh liked his wit. She was witty too, but she thought maybe he was a little faster, just a little. They sat down to dine at a small sidewalk café.

"What about our father?" he asked once they had ordered coffee.

"That part is complicated. There's just a lot more to all of it."

"What?"

"I brought along the letter for you to read," she said. "It's from our grandmother."

Everleigh pulled the envelope from her backpack and handed it to Bradley the same way she had once been handed this delicate information. He carefully pulled out the letter inside, unsure of what he was about to learn. It felt like a rite of passage almost. Everleigh knew it would explain a lot; it certainly would explain more to him than she could. She only knew what was in the envelope anyway, and he mostly did too, except for some unpleasant details, but now he would know those too. She hoped he would want to know. He quietly read the letter; Everleigh could almost tell which line he was reading at every moment. When he was done, he folded the letter, put it back into the envelope, and handed it back to Everleigh. He was quiet for some time and Everleigh was too.

"Wow," he said.

"Wow," Everleigh replied.

"That's a lot, isn't it?" he said.

"It is," Everleigh agreed. "I was so confused after I read it that I wasn't sure if I should try to find you, or if I wanted to find you, but my curiosity got a hold of me, so I tried to track you down and just knew I needed to do it. I'm glad you're here, and I'm glad you know now. It felt awful keeping you in the dark. Our mom didn't really want to keep either of us after the attack, but when she found out it was a boy and a girl, our grandparents convinced her to keep me, and mother eventually agreed."

They sat in silence for a while longer. Everleigh told him every detail of her trip to date. The good, the fantastic, the bad, the ugly, the neutral, and everything in between. He consumed every word. Even upon telling him things that had just happened, she found herself almost not believing it, like she was recounting a fairy tale and not her own memories. It *was* real, though. The food, the drinks, the friends, the hostels, the ferries, the seasickness, the massive awnings of ancient buildings all around her, the drum circle in Galway, the band doing the actual Full Monty inside a crowded pub. These were her memories now, and she knew she could cherish them all her life and share them again and again with others just as Grandma Susan had done with her.

Then it was Bradley's turn to share. He told her all about his childhood, growing up in Seattle, and his parents. She thought quietly to herself that he was the lucky one, being adopted into a warm and loving family, with two very present parents. Everleigh noticed she was still holding the letter in her hand, so she gently put it back into her backpack. They had a full meal and even more full conversation. *It is…easy,*Everleigh thought for maybe the hundredth time that day.

Like most first-time visitors to Paris, their first stop would be the Eiffel Tower. They were surprised by how big it seemed to them, even though, of course, they had seen pictures, including one of their grandmother smiling and posing with the Paris icon that Emily showed to Bradley. They found the approximate spot and then looked around for someone to take their picture; they didn't even have a chance to ask before someone approached them.

"Can I take your picture for you?" a kind-faced woman with a French accent asked them.

"Yes, please; that would be great. We're trying to get as close as we can to this," Everleigh said, showing the woman her photo.

"I see, yes. I can do that." The woman looked through the camera and again at the photograph. She took a few pictures and handed the camera and photo back to Everleigh.

"Thank you, so much."

"You are welcome. Who is that in the picture?"

"It's our grandmother."

"She's beautiful. I can see her in you. It's the eyes."

"I've heard that. That's kind of you to say."

Bradley and Everleigh stood there for a bit and looked at Grandma's picture again. Everleigh looked closely at Grandma Susan's eyes. There was a resemblance, and she found herself pleased with the thought. "Now, on for a closer tour of the tower," Bradley said as he motioned to the elevator and the patrons patiently waiting in line. Once at the summit of the tower, they braved the glass floor beneath them to soak in the romantic and mesmerizing views. Everleigh couldn't help but think of Stan, if only for a brief moment.

Once back on the ground, Everleigh and Bradley hailed a nearby taxi and took the picturesque six-minute ride along the Voie Georges Pompidou expressway to the Louvre Museum.

Everleigh was completely overwhelmed by the museum's mass. Not in a bad way, but in a way that let her know she could not experience it all in one afternoon. In fact, she surmised it was a three-day experience at a minimum. Everleigh and Bradley continued to what Everleigh thought of as the main attraction, the Mona Lisa, where there were so many tourists that they could not get anywhere near the painting. An older woman elbowed Everleigh in the side as she tried to get a closer look. So, Everleigh held her camera over her head and snapped a picture of the painting; then she handed her camera to her brother because he was taller than her, asking him to do the same. She figured it was the best way to go about it without getting elbowed by an old lady again. The painting was so much smaller than they had anticipated, yet still magnificent. They had filled up with enough art for the day, and as the sun began to set, and their shadows grew long, they walked to one of the many street-side cafés and ordered dinner and coffee, and chatted more about the family. It was some of the best food and bread Everleigh had tasted on the trip, and likely in her entire life.

Everleigh sat back and looked around, marveling that she was in Paris and her twin brother was sitting across from her. Everything around them was so big, loud, and packed with culture, architecture, and history.

Completely taken with the sights, Everleigh bought them tickets for a night boat cruise on the Seine River so they could see the city lit up. Going past the Eiffel Tower illuminated with gold lighting was a once-in-a-lifetime experience. By the "oohs" and "aahs" from fellow passengers, she assumed it was the same for most tourists. They spent the next days and nights taking in every inch of Paris that they could. It was crowded, busy, and happy. They saw the Louvre twinkling and glowing in the night air, which was a stunning sight to see. They visited the Arc de Triomphe and Notre Dame, and revisited the Louvre, then walked around the Moulin Rouge taking pictures.

After their visit of Paris was complete, Everleigh and Bradley jumped on a train to St. Malo, just over three-and-a-half hours to the west. It was a quaint, quiet city that offered a nice break from the hustle of Paris. A coastal city, the ocean was the most beautiful, clear green water Everleigh had ever seen. They ventured out for more sightseeing, including the St. Malo Castle and Old Town, a walled part of the city that had quite the nightlife. Inside the walled city there was music, dancing, food, and all-around excitement in the air. Everleigh and Bradley danced and sang to American songs while he twirled her around a very crowded walkway on the main path of the city. They ate fresh French crepes handed to them right off the griddle, and they tried a little of everything the vendors had to offer. What an extraordinary night! They were sad to see the night end and go back to their hostel inside the walled city.

The next day, after a train ride to Bordeaux, they found a hostel and checked in for the night. At the front desk, there was a brochure for a wine-tasting tour in nearby Saint-Emilion, so they decided that was where they would spend their final day together.

French wine country was a sight to behold. Saint-Emilion was one of the most picturesque wine villages in France. The tasting rooms were scattered about the small town, and their travels led them to the most popular stops. The wine was amazing, and most wine was served with paired food items to make the wine stand out and keep you from getting too drunk. They wanted to see the Monolithic Church of Saint-Emilion and its bell tower, which had stood out in the brochure they had seen before coming here. Its presence was gorgeous. The town was beautiful with churches and ruins. The streets were small, so they had to watch their steps on the cobblestone streets. They had some free time before the bus returned to Bordeaux, so Everleigh bought a few bottles of her favorite wine that they had tasted there and some sandwiches for a casual picnic in the afternoon sun.

After a fabulous time with new hope, food, wine, and great company, they remembered to raise a glass to Grandma Susan for being such an adventurous woman!

"To our next trip, whenever or *wherever* that may be," Bradley said as he raised his glass to Everleigh's. They sat for hours in the countryside, picnicking and drinking wine. When the wine was near its end, the sun broke through and glowed warmly through soft clouds as Everleigh's eyes filled with tears—the good kind, the kind that bring with them a sense of nostalgia. She took her last sip of wine and immediately thought to pull herself together.

Being here was like medicine for her soul. No matter what happened, she would be okay. *They* would be okay.

Bradley woke early the next morning and made espresso for them both. They had a brief window to chat before he had to leave. After more coffee, talking, and planning, they agreed Switzerland would be their next visit, whenever Bradley could get the time off from work again.

"I'm going to miss you," Everleigh said as they walked to the street to get a cab for him.

"I'm going to miss you, too."

They both choked up, knowing this would be the last time they would see each other for a while. Everleigh hugged her brother and waved as he rode off in a taxi to the Charles De Gaulle International

Airport. Then, she took a deep breath and walked back into the lobby to confirm her stay for a few more nights. She went back up to her room, her thoughts filled with Bradley's presence. She had a family. Even if they were apart, she knew they would always be there for each other.

Everleigh was nearing the end of the route her grandmother had taken, and she was only just now beginning to understand some things. She hadn't spent much time thinking about her mother until the incident on the train. While she wouldn't wish any sort of assault on anyone, it did help her understand why her mother had shut down after her rape. It had been a horrific experience that had made her mom feel weak and afraid. Everleigh had always loved her mother, but now she was beginning to understand how much her mother had loved her. It must have been so hard for her mother to think about how Everleigh had come into the world every time she saw her. It must have been so painful to see Everleigh and remember she had given up one of her children.

Everleigh began to think that even with such a violent start to life, her mother had loved her enough to do whatever she knew how to do to keep her safe. Yes, it had been overprotective and, ultimately, not the best thing, but it was all she could do.

"I love you, Mom, so much," Everleigh whispered to herself as she fell into the heaviest sleep she had known since she had first received the news of her mother's passing.

CHAPTER 16

The next two stops were the ones Everleigh had been truly looking forward to the most. Antibes and Monaco seemed so exotic and dreamy that she could hardly wait. She got up early the next morning and looked at her travel options. The way by train would take more than eight hours, but because Everleigh had been frugal, she realized she could afford to fly into Nice and grab a train to Antibes in half the time. She made her way to the airport, booked her ticket, and waited for her flight to be called. Arriving in Nice, she easily found the line for the train to Antibes.

She noted she could also easily catch a train from Antibes to Cannes eight miles away, something that sounded so exciting. The hostel was right on the water. She could hear the waves breaking on the shore as she got settled into her room. No question she was going to get into the swimsuit she had questioned packing back in Seattle.

Everleigh made her way to the beach and edged her way into water. She was used to colder water at home, so she braced herself for that initial chill. Nope! The water was so warm it was almost bath water. She quickly went all the way in, splashed around, and floated as best she could against the gentle waves. After about thirty minutes, she came out and spread out her towel to dry off and relax under the bright sun. She was on the French Riviera! She almost pinched herself to make sure it wasn't a dream.

Something like this, being in this place, was beyond a dream just several months ago. She wasn't sure how it would all play out, but Everleigh felt her life changing. And she was okay with that. She bought a salad and took her bottle of wine to the rooftop, which had plenty of tables, and watched the sun set. After the perfect day and swimming in the ocean, Everleigh slept long and sound that night.

The next morning, Everleigh looked forward to time on the beach after breakfast and then took a train to Cannes. When she arrived, she thought, *The energy is unreservedly different here in Cannes.* Her grandmother had written about her time there in her journal:

> *This is where all the movie stars hang out and premiere their wonderful films. It feels like if you're here, you're automatically creative. I could do anything here. I know I'll return home, but while I'm here, I will dream. Maybe I could be a photojournalist and take pictures of the glamorous movie stars as they arrive in limousines.*

Everleigh felt that same energy, and she felt a special bond with the grandmother she had never known. She took a few photos and imagined Grandma Susan doing the same thing. That creative energy was something they shared and something Everleigh hoped to embrace and nurture. She walked up the steps that were used by actors and actresses from around the world and tried to open the door to the theater, but to no avail; it was locked tight. She twirled around and imagined being there while some of her favorite actors entered the theater through the doorway. She took a few selfies and meandered down the walkway. Since it was a short trip back to her hostel, she waited for the last train. Then she again had dinner on the roof and watched the sun set.

She spent another day in Antibes, mostly on the beach, and she did a bit of sightseeing in Old Town. She bought her first few trinkets to help her remember this trip of a lifetime.

Everleigh realized she had loved every second of this trip, even the missteps, hassles, and doubts. It was all a part of her becoming who she was, and she was grateful for it all. She wondered how Grandma Susan could turn around and go back to Seattle after seeing all of this. That thought didn't have an answer, but Everleigh felt it would come to her when it was time.

In the morning, Everleigh packed up to grab a train to Monaco. She wanted to do some "touristy" things, including seeing the Prince's Palace that was built in 1215 as a border fortress of the Republic of Genoa. Here, her grandmother had managed to catch a glimpse of Prince Rainier; Everleigh wondered if she might see a royal as well. As she arrived at the palace, she caught the tail end of a convertible zooming around the corner and indulged the thought that it could be a royal. She was sure the person in the convertible, who waved at her, was Princess Stephanie, but Everleigh decided not even to try to get her camera out for a photo. Tourists probably did that every day, so she just enjoyed the wave.

After her "royal sighting," she decided to spend some time in the saltwater pool just below the palace. She rented an umbrella and an air mattress, changed into her swimsuit, and spent the day pretending she was one of the glamorous people. What a place this was with yachts— actual yachts—out on the water and spectacular homes dotting the beach. Everleigh knew many of the places, like the casino, were well beyond her budget. In fact, she learned from some fellow travelers at the hostel that there was a high-stakes fee even to get into the casino. No worries. It was more than enough to daydream on the beach, then take a city bus tour that had twelve stops, including the Japanese gardens and the Oceanographic Museum. She couldn't believe the spectacular views and the amount of wealth in Monaco. The city was full of tourists and casinos and so rich with history. Everleigh decided to stay a few extra days to enjoy the sights and feel the French Riviera's sun on her skin. She was looking forward to Italy, but she decided Monaco was worth the extra days.

It wasn't so much because it was Italy that she was looking forward to seeing it. It was because it was the last part of the trip her grandmother had made. Florence and Venice were the last two official stops; then it would be time to truly complete her quest—to get to Spain and Greece, the two countries Grandma Susan never visited.

Everleigh still wondered why her grandmother didn't just complete the trip and then go home. Surely her grandfather had loved her enough to wait a bit longer. Didn't he?

Despite it being nearly a five-hour trip, Everleigh decided to travel by train. The route went along the coast and would be an amazing scenic trek. There was a one-hour stop in Genova that nicely broke up the trip. Everleigh found a place to grab a bite to eat before getting back on the train to Florence. Once there, she made her way to the Accademia Gallery to see Michelangelo's David. It was at the end of a long hallway, but she could see it immediately. She recalled Grandma Susan's journal entry: "It's hard to imagine the great Michelangelo's hands actually touched, carved, and created this marble magnificence."

Grandma was right. David was magnificent and awe-inspiring. It was created between 1501 and 1504. That seemed so long ago, but the sculpture was still so amazing, so perfect. Everleigh noticed that the hands and feet were huge and out of proportion compared to the rest of the statue. She also noticed his butt was nice looking and she giggled to herself, wondering if her grandmother had thought the same thing. She spent the rest of the day walking around admiring all the art, small shops, and scenery. She found a place that served real Italian pizza and gelato, so she indulged in both.

By the time she got back to the hostel, Everleigh was ready for a nap, if not calling it a day altogether. She planned to head to Venice the next day, so skipping the search for nightlife was not a problem.

Venice was Everleigh's next stop. It was just a three-hour train ride, and Everleigh arrived mid-morning; the city had pathways throughout the small village, and she made her way around, taking lots of pictures. She immediately appreciated that it was almost impossible to get lost. She knew the entire city was surrounded by water, so if she just kept walking, she would end up back in town. Everleigh's sense of direction had greatly improved throughout her journey, but she was still nervous about getting lost in new places.

After checking into a hostel for the night, Everleigh made her way back to a deli she had passed by earlier. The smell of fresh bread and food was too enticing to skip. She bought some salmon, chicken, black olives, rosemary potatoes, and a beer. She easily found a quiet little corner and ate lunch in peace. It was a nice respite, and she garnered her strength for some night tourism. While no cars were allowed in Venice, lots of tourists were walking around enjoying the sights of the Venice canals. Everleigh noticed a great deal of activity along all the waterways, with water taxis zipping around the canals and gondolas everywhere.

She decided to get on a gondola and let someone else tour her around Venice. Grandma Susan had done the same thing, and Everleigh relished seeing the same places that likely had not changed much since the '50s. She saw the homes of Casanova and Marco Polo, cementing the fact that these were real people, not just characters in movies. She looked up as the gondolier pointed out the Bridge of Sighs. He explained that the bridge connected the courthouse to the jail. Its name stemmed from a popular belief that condemned prisoners would sigh with sadness as they were led through it to be executed.

The thought of people knowing they were going to their death reminded Everleigh of the concentration camps in Poland, which made her momentarily sad. Still, the beautiful canals cheered her up as night began to settle in. Gas lamps began to flicker and glow as she focused on photographing the stunning evening scenery.

The next day, Everleigh took a walking tour where she saw the Rialto Bridge, the Basilica of Santi Giovanni e Paolo, and the Church of San Pantalon with its beautiful ceilings. It took about two hours for the entire tour, so she filled up the rest of her afternoon checking out Venetian glass shops and scouting where she would eat dinner.

She ended up at a wonderful bacaro for cicchetti (the Venetian version of tapas), where she had her fill of countless small bites and great wine. Back at the hostel, she sat in the lobby reflecting on her journey. This was the last stop before Grandma Susan had returned home. She pulled out her last journal and turned to where the page had been torn in half. It read:

> *Tomorrow I was going to head for Spain. Today, I received his letter that he's home now and waiting for me. Before he left, he said he wanted to get married as soon as he got back. He came home sooner than we expected, but I am so grateful he's safe. Today's letter from Roger said, "I know this trip has been life-changing for you. I imagine we've both changed a lot and will have to get to know each other all over. I pray having a simple, quiet life is still going to be enough for you, and that you'll want that life with me."*
>
> *Oh, I have changed, so much. I feel stronger and more confident than I ever have. I know I don't have to have someone take care of me, but I do know I still love Roger. Perhaps an evening gondola ride will help me sort my thoughts.*

Here, the page had been torn in half, but Everleigh knew what it said. That little piece of journal paper had been tucked in an envelope along with Grandpa Roger's last letter. It was two sentences that had burned into her memory:

"It's clear now...Roger must come first. I'm going home."

CHAPTER 17

During the entire plane trip to Seville, Spain, Everleigh's head was filled with thoughts. She was trying to piece together her family history and everything that had led her to this point. It was clear that after that last gondola ride, Grandma Susan had decided to go back home to Roger. She had also written that she didn't need anyone to take care of her. What had made her decide to go then?

As Everleigh arrived in Seville, after her nearly three-hour flight, she thought to herself that Grandma Susan didn't miss much by skipping this place. It felt like just another large city with far too much noise and too much traffic. She didn't enjoy the feeling of it at all, but she made the best of it for a day and saw a few sights. Seville was a port town, large and very populated with stunning Roman architecture and the Seville Cathedral. Everleigh wished her grandmother had seen this beautiful church and taken a picture there. Thinking of her grandmother, Everleigh had someone take a photo of her in the doorway. The Seville Cathedral's Giralda Tower was 342 feet tall and just stunning. After all her sightseeing, Everleigh had a nice tapas dinner and went to bed early. She planned to leave the next day for Marbella. She knew little about it, but it had been on her grandmother's planned itinerary.

With a much shorter bus ride, Everleigh was heading toward the coast. She wasn't sure if it was her memory of Seattle or just the beauty of water, but Everleigh much preferred all her stops to be near the sea. Because she wanted to get out of Seville so quickly, she hadn't figured out where any hostels or hotels were, so she had no place to stay when she got there. She hailed a taxi and wondered if she should be worried that it was numbered "666." When she arrived in the town square,

153

where the driver assured her she could find a room, her fare was thirteen pesetas. She paid the driver, then walked through what she thought was an alley, which had a ladder she had to go under to get to her destination. What could have been bad luck must have been knocked out by the "triple threat" of three superstitious things because Everleigh did manage to find a room. It was a bit more expensive than she wanted to pay, but it was a nice hotel and a clean room. She took it.

The next day, Everleigh slept in a bit late, but she was out exploring again by mid-morning. Marbella was a pretty area, and the town square was dotted with statues by Salvador Dali. Everleigh began to appreciate his unique perspective on the world. It was nice to see some things beyond the more famous paintings she had studied in school. She took a mid-afternoon bus ride to the Rock of Gibraltar and had mixed feelings about the place. It was interesting, but again, very loud. She had no idea that cars could be driven on the "rock." It had monkeys running everywhere, jumping on cars, and jumping on tourists. Lots of people were taking their pictures with them, but after seeing a few of the monkeys get a bit mean, Everleigh opted out of that idea. She kept her distance and got back on the next bus back to Marbella.

Everleigh enjoyed Marbella and stayed there for a few days, relishing the beach and the sights. Then she decided to take the night train to Barcelona. After a long train ride, and an early arrival in Barcelona, she walked over to the La Rambla District, which she had heard from fellow travelers had some of the best food in the area. She knew they were completely unrelated, but she kept thinking of the song "La Bamba," which rattled in her head while she walked around the area.

When she checked into the hostel, the front desk clerk told her she was in a great central location for seeing the city, but he warned her there was a good deal of pickpocketing and other crime at night. Everleigh promised him, and herself, that she'd be careful. Eager to see the sights, Everleigh ventured to La Rambla, the central street in Barcelona, where she was met with mimes, some covered in gold, some in solid white paint, and slowly moving their bodies. As she passed by one of them, he came close to her and stopped, just staring and not moving. She got a little unnerved but stood there watching him, and eventually, she put a few dollars in his hat. He backed off a little once she gave him a tip. *What a curious profession*, she thought.

The sidewalk cafés were plentiful and all offered their take on tapas and sangria. Everleigh couldn't resist testing out several of the cafés, and she was feeling a little tipsy after a few sangrias. She walked all over the city taking photos of the architecture around Barcelona. Gaudi was a huge influence in the area, and his work was very distinctive and noticeable. Gaudi spent most of his life in Barcelona and most of his work had been created here, including the many years he spent working on the Sagrada Familia Basilica and several houses and other buildings in the area. In homage to Grandma Susan, Everleigh stopped at the Sagrada Familia Basilica, the largest unfinished church in the world. Its different eras were so noticeable in each architect's vision of this church. She was fascinated that they had started building it in 1882, but it wasn't scheduled to be finished until 2026.

Over one hundred years is quite the building schedule! she thought. *Even people working on it right now might not live to see the completed project.*

Everleigh then went to the Olympic Stadium, the site of the 1992 Summer Olympics. She couldn't get inside, but it was a huge stadium and she was able to take photos through the giant gates. She also walked across the Pont de Calatrava suspension bridge and took photos of the local sites.

Satisfied with all that she had seen in Spain, Everleigh caught a red-eye flight to Athens and arrived at 2:45 a.m. Passengers were shuttled to the terminal, which was so close she wondered why they didn't just walk. It was so late that no buses were running into town. She was thrilled to see a cab driver, who offered her a ride, but she didn't have the correct currency for the ride, or for checking into a hostel. Instead, she sat up most of the night in the airport because she wasn't sure of her surroundings or the neighborhood she was in. She was trying to stay awake and keep an eye on her bag. At first light, she headed out in search of an ATM.

After getting some local cash, Everleigh caught a bus into the Plaka District. She met a few men from Israel who were heading to a hostel and asked if she could tag along to see about a room there. Of course, they readily agreed and even helped her with her bag as they got off the bus and walked to the nearby hostel. There was one room left, a large co-ed room. Everleigh felt safe with her newfound friends, so they all agreed to take it; the boys took off for sightseeing while Everleigh took a much-needed nap.

When Everleigh woke up, she headed out to see the sights for herself, but she was in for a surprise. She had thought Athens would be one of the most beautiful places she'd ever seen, but to her shock, it wasn't. The first thing Everleigh noticed was that Athens was busy and loud. It was a true big city with lots of cars, buses, scooters, and other motorized vehicles cruising through the streets. Noise and exhaust flew at her from every direction. It was like New York, the city that never sleeps, except not as pleasant, charming, or energetic.

Everleigh had read about the historical areas in Athens and knew she couldn't leave without seeing those sights. She would have to stick it out and stay a few days in Athens. She already had the place to stay, and it wasn't expensive, so she set out to see what Athens had to offer. The first sight was the Parthenon, which was a former temple dedicated to the goddess Athena, and back in the mid-fourth century, BC, it had been used to serve as the city treasury. She chose to see this first because it was very visible from most of the city, sitting high on the hill. She made her way up to the majestic piece of art and giant marble columns that measured thirty-four-feet high and six-feet in diameter. The giant columns stood out across the city, and she saw in the guidebook that at night the building was lit up in gold. Everleigh took some photos by balancing her camera on rocks and using sticks to level it out. She had a small tripod, but it was wobbly on the rocks, so she opted for a more primitive "tripod" method. Just across from where the Parthenon stood was the Acropolis of Athens and the museum. She was able to hold several very heavy, solid, rock-etched items in her hands that were engraved with the year 400 BC. Athens' history made her realize how new the USA was, and she was so grateful to see and hold such history. As much as she wanted to see more history in Athens, she knew she wanted to spend as much of the time she had left in Europe on an island. She left the next morning for Santorini.

Everleigh knew Santorini would conclude her grandmother' trip.

Everleigh had written a handheld checklist, much like the one Grandma Susan had listing the cities she had visited. Everleigh's was longer since she had spent more time abroad and traveled to more cities. Greece was the last country to check off. She had waited until she was somewhere more beautiful than Athens to accomplish the small task of penning a checkmark next to Greece.

Arriving in Santorini, Everleigh was delighted to find a beautiful, vibrant island adorned with rugged cliffs and beautiful shores, truly a jewel she would thoroughly enjoy. A quaint little café by the ocean had the typical bright white and blue awnings. Although a "Help Wanted" sign was in the window, the place didn't seem all that busy. Everleigh took a seat outside the café as she breathed in the moist, salty ocean air and relaxed into a chair overlooking the water.

This must be what heaven feels like, she mused.

This was it—the perfect moment to check Greece off of her list, and she did just that. She felt immense satisfaction in such a small gesture, but the emotional significance of it was so much larger. Grandma Susan, wherever her spirit was resting now, could be satisfied in knowing that she had not only completed the homage to her, but she had done it all on her own.

Then, she had a bittersweet thought, *Now what?*

The trip would be ending, and Everleigh's grand adventure would be over. Just as quickly as she was satisfied about completing the trip, she was sad about it too.

"Do you need anything?" an older Greek woman asked her.

"I'd love some spanakopita," Everleigh replied, snapping out of her thoughts.

Either people like to sneak up on me or I am way too wrapped up in my own thoughts.

"I'll bring it right out," the woman said.

Several minutes later, a plate with the most beautiful-looking pastry, filled with delights, was on her table. The woman poured Everleigh some coffee and gave her a cool glass of ice water.

"Is this your first time to Greece?"

"Yes, it is. Is it that obvious?"

"No, just a lucky guess. What have you seen?"

"Nothing yet. I arrived early this morning."

"This is the *best* place to start. Our baklava is famous, the best in Greece."

"I believe it."

She left Everleigh to sit alone and bask in the afternoon sun. The woman, whom Everleigh learned was the café owner and named Diona, came back with more coffee and baklava, setting it on the table. Everleigh watched her walk back through the door, past the "Help Wanted"sign, but then Diona poked her head back out of the café.

"I see you were looking at my sign; are you looking for work?" she asked.

"Oh, no. I am just traveling through."

"It's a good job if you are interested," she said as if Everleigh had said nothing.

Everleigh happily brushed it off as she ate her fill of food, paid the bill, and went back to the hostel before exploring for the rest of the day.

The next morning, Everleigh found herself nervous and unable to focus, her mind preoccupied with the ending of her adventure and what she would do next. She walked to the shore and watched the waves instead of trying to do anything else. She knew she needed a moment simply to be. She knew things were changing for her. The air was sweeter, the sky was warmer, and she was stronger.

She had come out victorious. Life was about to start for her. This was a new day, and she was a new person!

"Thank you, Grandma Susan, for showing me how to be brave. Thank you, Bradley, for being a great friend and brother. Thank you, Everleigh, for allowing yourself this trip, for putting you first!" she said through tears of happiness as she watched the rhythm of the sea, which always calmed her. Entranced for what seemed like it could have been hours, her reverie was interrupted by a young Greek teenager, the one who managed the front desk of the hostel where she was staying. He walked up to her to let her know she had a phone call waiting for her.

CHAPTER 18

Everleigh went inside to take the call in the lobby, assuming it would be Bradley on the other end, phoning to let her know he had made it back to the States safe and sound. It wasn't. It was Stanley, the attorney. *Her* attorney. Hearing his voice made her heart leap in ways it never had. She had thought of him throughout this trip more often than she wanted to, but she was proud of herself for waiting until he called her, and now, she had something to speak with him about and had emailed him earlier in the day to let him know where she was staying.

"Everleigh?" he said, sounding pleasantly surprised. "Everleigh Ford?"

"Hi, Stan. Yes, it's me, Everleigh," she replied, reminding him he could be casual with her.

"Well, well, well...."

Everleigh giggled. She had forgotten how much she liked the sound of his voice.

"How are you?" he asked. "Are you headed back to Seattle now? It's just about time for you to come back here, isn't it?"

"Stanley, what this trip has taught me is to live without worries and in the moment, and I am so proud of myself for allowing me to do just that. So, I plan to stay in Greece a bit longer. I truly hope you understand?"

"I think I do," Stanley awkwardly said.

After a few moments of thought, Stan asked, "Have you made a decision on the house?"

"I've decided to sell the house."

"What? Are you sure?"

"I am sure, and I'll need your help. I want you to go through the will and the house and see if there's anything—any assets that can be shared with Bradley, and I'd like to arrange for him to go to the house before the sale; there may be things that he would like to have. I want to split everything I have with him."

"Everleigh, you don't have to do that."

"I know, but I want to, and I trust Bradley. Have him keep anything he wants, and we can sell or donate the rest."

"That's very generous of you and, of course, I can help you. It's ultimately your decision…." He paused.

"Are you sure about the house?" he asked.

"Yes, I am sure. I want to stay in Greece. I may not stay here forever, but this is what I want."

"Greece, huh? That sounds nice."

"I'm on Santorini Island, and it's the most beautiful place I've ever seen."

"Everleigh…" he started; his voice sounded small.

It pulled at Everleigh's heart since she was hopeful about what he would say next.

"We've only just found each other, and now you want to live with an ocean between us?" he said.

"It won't be forever, just for now. They have phones in Europe, remember?"

"I do remember," he said. "I just don't know if that's enough."

Everleigh could feel the tug-of-war in her heart, knowing that she wasn't ready to go back to Seattle, but wishing she could be with Stan all the same. This was her new beginning, and she knew if this was what she felt it was, he would understand.

"There are other ways of keeping in touch, I suppose," he said.

"There are," she said, but then she realized she wasn't sure what he meant. "How?"

"Oh, you know, email, letters.... I suppose I'll need an address to get you any paperwork that will require your signature once you find a permanent one."

"Sure. I don't know where that will be yet, but I'll let you know when I know."

"I know where you're staying now," said Stan.

Everleigh's heart doubled in size, and she nearly fell out of her chair.

He wants to come here and see me.

"I knew your office had a courier service," she said, "but I didn't think they came all the way across the Atlantic."

"I'm ready when you are, Everleigh," he replied.

Stan had to jump off their call for a client meeting, but he promised to make sure everything went smoothly with the sale of the house and that she would be kept informed every step of the way. Everleigh found herself positively beaming from ear to ear, a smile she never knew she was capable of. Deep down in her soul, she knew she was speaking to the man she would marry, no matter how far off that might be; she just knew, and that brought her a comfort unlike anything she'd experienced to date.

The next day, morning came early, and Everleigh knew exactly what she had to do, with a future broad and wide-open in front of her, it was so obvious.

She marched up the road from her hostel and over the hill to her now favorite beachside café. She called for Diona, walked inside, and removed the "Help Wanted" sign from the window.

ABOUT THE AUTHOR

Donna Rodrigues was born and raised in Santa Monica, California. In college, she studied art and photography. She later moved to Seattle where she lived for seventeen years. Donna's enthusiasm for travel grew after biking and backpacking through sixteen European countries for six months by herself.

Now, with thirty countries under her belt, she has written her debut novel, *Finding Everleigh*, a tale of travel and adventure mixed with the ups and downs of being alone. She is currently working on her next book, *The Mysterious Mysteries of Mr. Ri*, a fun-loving story about her orange and white tabby who loves adventure.

As an avid lover of the outdoors, Donna began taking photographs, making abstract oil paintings, and helping animals at a very young age. Rescuing and keeping the dogs and cats she rescues is her forte. When she's not writing, she can be found taking photos of nature, animals, and children locally and abroad. She also stays busy cycling, traveling, and gardening.

Donna currently lives in Long Beach, California with her husband and her three rescued dogs and two cats.